ILLUSIVE LEGEND

Warren DeVere Stephens

First edition

PUBLISHED by DeMore

2021

ISBN 978-1-7376770-3-1

The intoxication of fame and fantasy can become obsessive, vaulting a young boy or girl into the realities of adulthood.

Unfortunately, the consequences of adult choices are often more harsh than those of childhood.

TABLE OF CONTENTS

CHAPTER 1

SCHOOL DAYS

Eyes front!" Bellows the scrawny bent over man.

Craack! The three-foot oak pointer slams a desk, adding an exclamation point to his command. "You pay attention or you'll get a taste of this pointer to wake you up."

The one-room schoolmaster, Mr. Henry Barrow, or "Sarge," is not happy. His underwhelming patience is worn so thin newsprint could be read through it. It's mid-afternoon, the schoolroom is warm and youthful attention wanes. The long oak pointer, a fixture in Sarge's right hand, is an effective way to recapture inattention. Striking the desk is shocking but a great deal less painful than when the pointer is used to mete out individual punishment should Sarge believe it's warranted. A swat across the back of legs or across the shoulder is universally feared but mostly experienced in reality by the older boys.

But like it or not, Sarge is the schoolmaster. To his young charges he is investigator, prosecutor, judge and disciplinary executioner inside the one-room school in Cornwall, Missouri. Sarge is missing his left arm at the shoulder, and just as noticeable is the pink as a baby's bottom, two by six inch crudely stitched strip of hairless skin on the left side of his head. Both are compliments of battle-wounds. If he could stand up straight, which he can't, Sarge would be even more imposing at over six feet tall, skinny and awkward.

Anyone familiar with the Washington Irving story the "Legend of Sleepy Hollow" would likely see Sarge as the personification of Ichabod Crane. Perhaps Sarge sees his appearance differently because he swirls a straggle or two of dark greasy hair in a rather ingenious way attempting to cover the nasty scar and his very pink scalp. He has a big hook nose, pointy chin and pronounced Adam's apple. He doesn't shave every day, so he sometimes appears as if he's coming off a bender, which is not altogether out of the question according to community rumors. He has thick, dark eyebrows that slant down toward his nose, so he naturally appears angry. Perhaps the eyebrows are not a deceptive look because he is angry and disagreeable most of the time, so his physical features fit his personality package very well.

He wears old dark blue wool uniform trousers every day, shiny in the seat and around the pockets from repeated overuse and the cleanliness is questionable unless he washes them on the weekends. Every day at school Sarge picks one of his wardrobe's two shirts, and originally they must have been white, but the harsh, lye laundry soap and the uniform trousers as a washtub partner have created a sickly yellowish tone to the shirts. Suspenders help keep the shirt tucked into the trousers. Sarge's rough appearance is accentuated by the acrid odor of poor personal hygiene.

The school is run according to Sarge's frequent use of military jargon as if the cherub-like rosy faces of innocence in front of him are hardened warriors about to be directed and cajoled into battle. Students fear Sarge and his pointer, but there is a glimmer of daily hope. On rare occasions when his physical pain or perhaps his thirst for a drop of medicinal alcohol gets too severe, he lets school out early. When that occurs, students run from the school like it's on fire because, even though it's never happened, there's the odd chance Sarge's pain might suddenly subside, he'd change his mind, chase everyone down with that pointer and make them march back to school for more inspired education.

Local people say when Sarge was growing up he was hot-tempered and mean-spirited. Many thought it would do him good to join the army. The most popular part of encouragement for Henry to do his patriotic duty was that he'd be gone for a long time. And so Henry Barrow joined the Union Army and left Cornwall.

The respite of Henry Barrow's sabbatical from town didn't last as long as hoped. He was severely wounded in of one of his many skirmishes in the War Between the States. He survived, was awarded a battlefield promotion to Sergeant but lost his left arm at the shoulder and was provided a metal plate implanted to stabilize a large missing piece of his cranium. But doctors' surgeries couldn't repair, and likely exacerbated, Barrow's mean streak that lies well beneath the metal plate.

Sarge is doubly bitter now because he was mustered out as unfit for further duty in the Grand Army of the Republic, the Union. He spent a year being shipped from one military hospital to another because he had fits of violent and irrational behavior. So when Sarge was officially mustered out of the army and returned to Cornwall, it just happened that the Cornwall School was without a schoolmaster or mistress, so Sarge applied. When the school board told him he was hired, he responded with a sadistic laugh and said that he could whip these little ruffians into shape, including those heathen Irish and "the little bastards" from rebel sympathizer families. Apparently, the school board felt the main qualification was based more on his willingness to take the job rather than his planned curriculum.

So here in Sarge's classroom today sits sixteen year-old Michael Sean O'Day (Mickey). Like the other students he's fighting boredom, trying his best to avoid the dreaded pointer and hoping to escape the rigors of this day's educational experience. He's confident he can appear alert and engaged with the school master while mentally a universe away vividly picturing himself as a celebrated war hero. Mickey doesn't trust or like the school teacher, and Sarge makes no bones about his dislike for Mickey and Mickey's brothers and sisters. He is not fond of Irish people and he hates rebel sympathizers, both of which the O'Days are guilty.

Mickey is of slight build at five feet five and close to one hundred ten pounds. He's been weighed on a cattle feed scale at the livery and that's close enough. He is surprisingly strong and not an ounce of fat anywhere. He moves with a fluidity that is often seen in natural gifted athletes. But that athletic, yet slim body holds all the distinctive trademarks of a complete Irishman. He has fiery red hair, fair complexion, and freckles. His face is round and when he smiles his facial features are disarmingly angelic.

Mickey's school clothes, work clothes, and Sunday clothes are all the same clothes. The only time there's any different clothes is when there's a chance to swim in the Castor River. Then there are no clothes. Like the other six O'Day children, clothes are generally clean but ill-fitting and threadbare. Rarely is there a first-generation shirt, pants or pinafore. But infrequently there are a few items made from colorful, printed, cotton feed sacks. Trips to the livery become spirited family competition over who gets to pick a feed sack print when "new" clothing may be in the future. At school with Mickey are his younger sisters and brothers, Aileen, Bronagh, and Caireann, Ailbe, Breandan, and Coilin. They make up the ABC O'Day boys and the ABC O'Day girls, as kids refer to them at school.

These are tough times in Southeastern Missouri and for Missouri overall. Missouri is neither a true southern state nor is it a true northern state; neither is it an eastern state nor a western state. It's in the midst of the country, and many of its residents are one or two generations removed from European immigration. In the entire state, there are only a handful of large farms that have slaves, so the issue of the war being fought over slavery is far from anything heartfelt, debated or experienced. It's a state that is pulled hither, and yon since part of its populace sympathize with the United States and its Union Army and another large but often silent contingent of secessionist supporters of the Confederate States of America and the Confederate Army. Some communities are like a powder keg with a lit fuse, but people in the Cornwall area try to stay to themselves and avoid conflicts unless something about the war is rubbed under their noses. Deep loyalties and nasty feelings are obvious when a family's loved one is killed, sent home maimed like Sergeant Henry Barrows or simply appears for a short furlough.

Many a young man has been wooed by the siren's song of war as they watch their parents eek out a hand to mouth existence on a small farm, hear about the war, see how people ooh and ahh at men in uniforms, and dream about the glamour of soldiering. Off they go, and the parents become dyed in the wool supporters of whichever army is chosen. It's almost like the more you support the cause of the side where your relatives are fighting, you add layers of protection for the loved one's safe return. Shallow logic, but familial patriotic commitments are to the bone marrow!

In Cornwall, people generally know the side of one's allegiance but there are goods to be bought and sold, there are children who need to go to school, there are things best left unsaid outside one's own doorstep. So, there's a delicate thin facade of peaceful coexistence in public settings but fear and anger smolder beneath the surface.

Reminders of the war happen a couple times a month when various size units and patrols from both armies pass through Cornwall, advancing or retreating, chasing or evading, deserting and running. Often they simply appear at someone's farm. The soldiers are tired, hungry and irritable, so depending on the discipline and leadership, soldiers from both sides can be crude and savage. The first contact is often by the woman of the household, and she tries her best to convince the soldiers that this is a struggling farm whose menfolk are away supporting whatever army is standing there nose-to-nose at that moment. Sometimes the housewife is convincing, sometimes not. Sometimes it makes no difference for those bent on taking what they want without regard to the slightest degree of conscience. More than a few times officers direct their troops to confiscate farm animals, butcher them on the spot and completely strip crops or gardens. There are tales where soldiers are part of small bands, so-called raiders, and they represent terror. Sometimes everything of value is stolen, occupants murdered and farm buildings burned. Cornwall has been spared murder and general terror but everyone universally lives in fear that it could happen to anyone…anytime.

Cornwall, Missouri is south of Fredericktown, the Madison County seat, and it's primarily a small railroad station and a one-street town with one of each type of commercial necessity. There's a general store, a blacksmith and livery, a six-room hotel and sometimes restaurant, a barbershop with twice a week poker in the back and a saloon with reputed upstairs entertainment. There is a sheriff, but no sheriff 's office. A windowless storeroom in the livery stable is used on occasion as the sheriff's jail cell. The sheriff, Benny Spielhagen, keeps the peace because he's big enough to manhandle an errant man and have a personal "talk" in the one room cell. Big Benny's methods have worked just fine in Cornwall.

The O'Day's small farm is about a mile from the school and the town. Like many hand-to-mouth small farmers, the O'Day spread has zero hints of prosperity with its dilapidated two-story wood house and a weathered, partially propped -up barn nestled among the weeds beyond the garden. The livestock consists of three

Jersey milk cows, a brood of ten skinny pigs, three horses, a mule, and a couple dozen chickens. The milk, occasional fried chicken, eggs and garden vegetables assure the eight family members at home don't go hungry but Mickey and his Ma are the only real workers and deterioration of the buildings is outpacing their seldom maintenance efforts.

As far back as he can remember, Mickey's dad, Peter, drank a lot and disappeared into town frequently so the O'Day family was accustomed to poverty. Peter left four years ago to prospect for gold in California with assurances of the gold rush, promising wealth so he could send for the family. The family never heard from him again. Mickey's older brother Joe took up the family leadership reins, worked the small farm and for extra money helped on other farms when he could.

But after Peter abandoned the family, Joe seemed to be cut from the same cloth as his Pa. Except, Joe always had cash. The family never knew the depth of Joe's pockets but he always had enough to take care of his family and his own personal weaknesses. Part of the extra money regularly disappeared in the saloon and on the barber's poker tables. But Joe also earned money by prizefighting once a month and as his success as a fighter grew he had local financial backers who accompanied Joe to other area towns. They wagered. Joe fought any takers. Joe never lost, and he was popular with most everyone, but Joe disappeared one day and left a simple note that he was to be a Rebel soldier. His popularity waned as mention of his name in town was somewhat of a lightning rod. Yankee sympathizers in Cornwall no longer mention him, but most local people on both sides of the political split are well aware of the new and growing reputation of Corporal Joe O'Day as a Rebel Army hero.

Mickey is very aware of Joe's reputation, and he hears about it at school either in the sarcastic comments of Sarge or taunts from other students who reflect their parents' political alliances. Mickey's ma also reminds him every day how great Joe is and how much he's missed at home. Barely a day goes by without Mickey being reminded to work a little harder so he can chase Joe's shadow around from farm chore to farm chore. Mickey certainly admires and loves his older brother, but between going to the unpleasant atmosphere in school every day and hurrying home to do chores, Mickey burns like white-hot phosphorus with a desire to prove himself as a man, as a soldier and as a hero.

He simply needs the opportunity to prove himself but he's thwarted at every turn by his required chores to herd the kids home from school, feed the livestock, gather eggs and shovel the never-ending manure out of the barn.

Mickey ends each night going to sleep with his proclamation, "If I wait for someone to help me, I'll be doing this forever. Nobody's gonna help. Not Joey. Not Mama. Nobody, except me. Michael Sean O'Day."

Mickey is one-hundred percent certain he too could be a popular hero, as a good prizefighter and soldier if given a chance.

But Mickey's dreams disappear into daily reality of doing chores at home and defending himself at school. It's a sad scene to see boys from dirt poor families picking fights over their parent's politics, but pubescent boys with spoon-fed political poison from home, encouraged at school to act out those opinions and ever-present testosterone seldom produce a surprising result. At this afternoon's recess Mickey doesn't respond at first to snide comments but when very hurtful things are said about his family and their Irish heritage he can't let it slide. One thing leads to another, and he finds himself in a direct challenge to fight.

The next day, five-foot-five, one-hundred -ten pound Mickey O'Day is again the bullying object of the much bigger sixteen-year-old, Elmer Hoenisch. Elmer is not six feet tall but close enough that another year or so will make the mark. He likely weighs in nearly a hundred fifty or sixty pounds, broad shoulders and like most kids of this region, and the progeny of farm work, not any fat.

Elmer and two of his friends corner Mickey by the school building at the afternoon recess, and he's stepping up the ante to fight Mickey after school.

"Hey, O'Day, is everybody in your family as stupid as you look? You should roll your pants up a little more in case you gotta run away when yer stealin potatoes on your way home. And that sissy shirt. Look at it boys. Who but a stupid mick Irishman would wear something like that? Oughta be a dress for one of yer stupid sisters or maybe a dress fer you, ya thievin Irishman."

Mickey is quick with his retort to Elmer, "You better shut up. I ain't afraid of you."

Elmer laughs with delight because he's drawn Mickey into it, and he knows it. "Oooh, I'm pissin myself from fear and shakin in my boots. O'Day, you're a yellow-belly reb coward just like your brother."

" You better shut yer pie hole! My brother, Joey ain't no coward and I ain't either."

"Yeah, well my Pa says one of these days your whole family's gonna get strung up for being traitors. Your brother was too much a Mama's boy to get in the real army…the Union."

"I'm warning you Hoenisch. You better shut your mouth or yer gonna get it shut for ya."

Elmer laughs, "Yeah. Sure. I'll be waitin for ya after school less yer too scared."

Mickey is so angry his mouth is dry, and he has tears in his eyes. He really doesn't want to fight Elmer because Elmer's so much bigger. Worst of all he'll likely have to fight two or three boys, not just Elmer. Mickey opts for what is best at the moment, and he heads back inside the schoolhouse to get away from immediate trouble on school grounds.

As Mickey silently turns to go inside, Harry Britton, one of Elmer's friends, trips Mickey and he stumbles his way up the steps toward the door. But Mickey tries to act as if it's no problem and he takes two awkward steps, and in the door he goes. His heart is racing. He'll be lucky if everyone just goes home after school, but it will not surprise Mickey to see these guys waiting for him off the school grounds and just down the road.

When school turns out for the day, all the kids with more energy than they had coming to school this morning, start on their paths home and Mickey. His brothers and sisters are no different.

This afternoon Mickey's nervously looking around to see if Elmer and his friends will go on home or if they will try to start trouble again. Mickey doesn't have to wonder very long. The O'Day clan barely clears the low split rail fence that marks the end of school property when he hears Elmer's voice from behind. Mickey looks back and sees Elmer, Harry and Ted walking a quick pace to catchup to the O'Days. Mickey is at the rear of his group of brothers and sisters and he slows his pace so if there's a face off it will be sooner than later and the other kids won't be involved.

"Look boys it's the yellow-bellied Reb. You better run to your old lady and hide under her apron, you red-headed Irish scum. I know you're a coward and traitor just like your mick brother. He's gonna get his ass shot off anyways cause he'll be running away from any real fighting."

Mickey drops his books and turns to face the trouble. As his brothers and sisters pause at the commotion, Mickey directs them, "Go on. You kids get on home. Don't stand gawkin at me, get goin. This is somethin I gotta do. Run home! And not a word to Ma. You hear?"

No need to answer out loud. Mickey's brothers and sisters take off for home, eyes wide with fright but doing what their older brother tells them. Suddenly it's clear to Mickey that this fight is going to happen and likely all three will attack him.

Elmer, Harry and Ted don't take long until they're confidently close. All afternoon Mickey's been thinking how he'll handle this confrontation should it take place so now it's showtime. He's going to fight like Joe taught him. Don't put your fists up at first, just turn a little to the side so you can't get hit square in the stomach. Just act like you're going to argue and not fight, but when the troublemaker's face is within arm's length, strike first and as hard as you can. Try to surprise your opponent. Center your fist on the nose and upper lip. If the hit is first and strong enough it can bring the fight to a quick halt. It's about surprise, hitting first, and hitting hard.

Mickey can't even hear the insults being hurled at him as Elmer gets closer and closer, looking more confident with every step. Mickey must appear defenseless to Elmer and the others for the surprise to work, but Mickey must hit first like Joe taught him. Mickey's looking at that big, soft Hoenisch nose with nostrils flaring in and out as Elmer feels on firm ground in his role as chief bully. Mickey keeps his hands to his side, palms up almost as if already deferring to Elmer. Mickey is estimating his own arm length and zeroing in on his target. Mickey takes a deep breath. That's it, Elmer, just a half step closer. Just a little closer. Elmer obliges' moving closer, and closer to Mickey. Elmer is enjoying the bravery of his own voice and the lack of response to his taunts. Elmer's friends are laughing and slapping each other on the back already celebrating Elmer's apparent victory.

The time is right, and without any warning or words, Mickey strikes. He lands his fist hard and fast to Elmer's inviting beak. It sounds like smashing a fist into a bucket of thick cream with a snap enveloped by a slushy sound. Mickey is even surprised at the sound.

Elmer gasps in shock, stumbles back a step and then drops forward to his knees and bending down with his forehead almost touching the ground in front of Mickey's shoes. Mickey takes a step back, both fists raised, glaring in silence at Ted Glaser and Harry Britton.

Mickey can tell by their expressions that no one else wants what Elmer received, so Mickey takes another deep breath and quietly issues a challenge, "Who else? "

Elmer's friends don't need to answer out loud. They are spectators and didn't come for a walloping like Elmer just received. Ted bends down and tries to help Elmer to his feet, but Elmer outweighs Ted by fifty pounds, so Ted drops Elmer. Elmer gives a loud groan and turns his face looking for help. His nose and lips are bleeding.

Mickey's immediate trouble is over just like that. Harry steps in to help Ted and the two of them struggle to lift Elmer by supporting under his arms, and they turn around and walk the other way slowly with a beaten and embarrassed Elmer. Not a word is said to Mickey, but he can hear Elmer sobbing as he is helped toward home.

Mickey picks up his books, makes a cautionary glance over his shoulder and walks toward his own home. If he's lucky, Sarge may not even find out about this. If Elmer or Elmer's parents complain to Sarge, Mickey will surely get the schoolmaster's wrath at school. Mickey hurries home. Boy oh boy, Joe sure would be proud of him.

Just like Joe always says, "We're Irish, and we're tougher than any half dozen of these other mutts. You just gotta know when and how to fight."

Mickey smiles as he thinks of Joe and says out loud what he'd love to be saying to Joe right at this instant, "Okay Joey, I'm Irish, I can fight, and I can stand shoulder to shoulder with you as a soldier. We're O'Days, and we can whip anything or anybody. I can be a hero just like you, Joe...or even better."

After a quarter hour walk across a pasture, the O'Day dogs come to greet Mickey. The wagging tails and the barks of greeting make Mickey feel happy, nearly forgetting the altercation with Elmer. As Mickey reaches the steps up to the porch, Mickey's ma comes out the screen door, hands on hips.

"Jesus, Mary, and Joseph, Michael Sean, the way the kids told it you was about to get a whumpin over by the schoolyard. I was about to put supper off the stove and come lookin for ya. Are you okay?"

"Yeah, Ma. I'm fine. Elmer Hoenisch has been pickin at me all day yesterday and today, and he said some stuff about Joe bein a coward and us bein Irish scum. I don't take that crap from nobody."

Watch your mouth, Michael Sean. You got little kids a listenin...so then what?"

So Elmer and two more of em were waiting for me after school to test me out, and I did what Joey taught me. There was only two hits. I hit the Elmer in the nose, and he hit the dirt. Fight over."

"But it wasn't in school or on school grounds was it?"

"Nope. Off school grounds but I just hope no one tells Sarge. He'd love to pick on me about us supportin the rebs."

Mickey's ma makes a sigh of relief and opens her arms for a hug. Mickey obliges her, and she says softly to him, "Mickey, I love ya son. Glad ya didn't get roughed up. Now you got chores to do cause we aint got the luxury of havin a man around to take care of everything. So you scoot on and get yer stuff done before supper. Ya know neither of youse boys are trouble-makers, but Lord knows we Irish are always havin to defend ourselves and just between you and me I'm glad you punched that son-of- a-buck."

Now Mickey feels like he got punched in the stomach. Every single responsibility falls to him and yet in his ma's eyes he's just a little kid. She may have meant well but her words cut Mickey deeply as he repeats in a whisper, "No man around to take care of things."

His confidence is compressed back into his small body but that fuels his obsession about his destiny with heroism. He dutifully goes toward the barn. He looks to the sky, turning his head from side to side in frustration and says aloud, "No man around, huh? Well, what about me? I'm Michael Sean O'Day and I am a man. I am a man. One of these days, real soon…they'll all see. Everyone will know the name Mickey O'Day! "

CHAPTER 2

THE DOWNSIDE OF VICTORY

The next day at school Elmer is the topic of conversation. He's sporting a purple, swollen nose and bruising under both eyes from the trauma to his nose. Sarge moves toward the rear of the classroom and comes over in front of Elmer, bends down a little and looks at his face from side to side. The room is as silent as a crypt, and though Sarge speaks quietly it's certain he's asking Elmer what happened. Mickey can't hear all of the conversation, but the word "reb" is included. Sarge walks to the front of the room, turns slowly and looks directly at Mickey.

Mickey is bound to be the day's entertainment by way of the oak pointer. Sarge may be in the front of the room but that's only a couple of long Sarge-steps from Mickey. Staring, pointer in hand, lightly tap, tap, tapping it on his desk. Mickey's heart is beating in high tempo expecting that pointer to soon find its way to his face and shoulders. It seems like a silent eternity with certain results.

Instead of the expected lunging steps and the pointer across the shoulder, Sarge moves slowly staring directly in Mickey's eyes. When he's directly in front of Mickey he bends down and almost whispering says, " Well, well. We have a dirty, little bushwhackin reb in our midst. So ya took Elmer by surprise and figured nobody would find out, huh? Well, I'm goin over to talk to Elmer's dad after school and we'll see if he can figure a way to break you of that sort of bad habit. I'd go talk to your pa but of course you ain't got one, do ya?"

Then Sarge gets so close to Mickey's face he can smell the bad, whiskey breath as Sarge whispers, "Dirty Reb. Kinda like breakin an egg-suckin dog but this time you're gonna get the lesson and real good."

Sarge stands erect, takes a deep breath, walks to the front of the class, turns facing everyone and talks in a very reserved tone of voice, "I know things are said or things happen and it sometimes takes rough stuff to settle a problem. I also know that boys are boys. But today, boys and girls, I want you to listen very carefully to me. Our great country is being torn apart by an army of rebellious traitors and a few of our local people who are traitors as well. We cannot just let this war drag on and on and bleed our republic dry. So boys, don't waste your time scuffling or punching a schoolmate. That's a waste of your young healthy bodies and minds. The rebels will all get justice one day real soon. Every stinkin one of em. "

Then he continues, "We've got to whip this rebel army once and for all time. We have to round up the people who support the rebels, get them in prison and a good many of them hanged as traitors. Now you say, "Well what can I do? I'm too young."

Sarge continues,"And here's the answer. I know the enlistment age to be a soldier for the Grand Army of the Republic is eighteen but I dare say there are many lads who are as young as eleven or twelve who are doing their duty to defend our country. I ask each of you boys to go home tonight and ask your pa and ma if they could spare you for this righteous cause. All of you are under eighteen, but there is a handful of you boys who are fifteen and sixteen. You'd be used as buglers, drummers, help in the hospital, clean guns…a whole lot of beneficial and useful ways to help the cause until you're eighteen and old enough to be a complete soldier. I'd rather see you helping the brave Union soldiers by helping, fighting or even killing for your country than fighting in schoolyard scraps. If, at the moment, you have to even a score, so be it. But then that's enough. Look to a bigger cause. A righteous cause. See if your pa and ma will let you join the great Union Army. If the answer is yes, come and tell me, and I'll personally get you to the area recruiting officer and see that you get in. Now. Time for schoolin'. Eyes Front!"

Clear enough Sarge's message is for most everybody in the classroom except the O'Days. That is, except the part about evening a score. Mickey glances at Elmer but he likely doesn't want to risk another punch on his beak. Mickey's not sure what Elmer's pa will do if Sarge goes and talks to him but maybe he won't even go. But there are some of Sarge's words that actually could apply to the Confederate cause as well so Mickey is going to ask his ma if he can go join his brother Joe in the Confederate States of America Army. She'll for sure say no and probably whack him one for even asking. But he's going to ask.

Rest of the day, Elmer, Ted and Harry stare at Mickey but keep their distance. Mickey feels even more confident now. If only Joey could see him. They will all stay away from him from now on.

The next day after school, the band of seven O'Days is sauntering slowly out of the school grounds and along the dirt road toward home. Another spring day with the warm sunshine and soft breeze. The smell of freshly turned earth in a nearby field and the humid air add to the energetic feeling of being out of class. Not much is being said, but if the little O'Day kids are like Mickey, they are thinking of getting home and having a warm meal after chores. The road narrows into a one-lane wagon path as it enters a dense thicket of sumac bushes and oak trees on both sides of the road. Sometimes the sun is blocked as they walk through this part of the trip home and the kids call it the enchanted forest. Tired from school and anxious to get home, none of the kids see the figure suddenly emerge close behind Mickey. It's the sound that causes all the heads to jerk in shock and fear boils over, erasing any enchantment that may have been.

Swak! Swak! The hissing sound of a walking cane slicing through the air and striking its target, the neck and head of Mickey.

The sound alone makes the children gasp and squeal. The girls scream as they see their older brother, Mickey, crumple to the ground.

The man standing over Mickey is Harry Hoenisch, Elmer's older brother, and he's struck Mickey by surprise. Harry meant to come down in a chopping motion on Mickey's head but missed and hit him primarily on the neck and collarbone.

Mickey crumples in agony and then, grimacing from pain, begins to roll over to see what's happening. His brothers and sisters aren't waiting around, and they run for home, screaming. Mickey's by himself, and it's not just Harry. Elmer makes his appearance from the roadside. Harry, who's home from the war with a leg wound, convalesces at home until he can return to duty. He walks with a limp and uses a cane and now Mickey's personally familiar with the cane, a stained hickory stick with a metal knob on the top.

"Okay, little Reb, let's see how tough you are."

Harry flips the cane around in his hands with the knob downward as he slashes it across Mickey's legs. He follows it with a glancing blow to Mickey's head. Suddenly it's like a dream and Mickey can hardly see his attackers. Everything looks dark and without color. Harry and Elmer's voices sound like they are echoing. Mickey flashes back to being allowed to climb down inside a new cistern they built at home and how all the voices down inside it echoed. He's dazed and losing consciousness as the cane strikes again and again. First on his ribs and as he rolls over to his knees a solid blow beneath one arm. The pain in his side is excruciating, and the sound is an unbelievable drum-like hollow sound. Mickey falls face first and passes out.

It's as if time is an illusion. Mickey begins to regain consciousness, and he's totally confused. He cannot guess what happened or how long he's been unconscious. The pain is so intense he tries to edge back to sleep but can't. He can't breathe. As Mickey moans his way awake and tries to look around and breathe, he's aware that Harry is sitting on his back. As Mickey groans again, Harry grabs Mickey's hair and pulls his head up and back.

"C'mon Elmer. Anything you'd like to say to this Irish mick before I give him a little more lesson in Union Army?"

"Yeah, I have something I wanta say."

Elmer kicks Mickey a glancing blow in the face with his boot and Mickey blacks out again.

Once again the length of time is a mystery before Mickey slowly begins to wake. He's not sure how long he's been lying here, but the pain is worse than anything he's ever encountered. Oh, how he hurts all over! It's quiet and getting dark. Mickey is confused about all that just took place, and he's not even sure where he is. He pushes up with his arms raising his chest, but he cannot get high enough to see above the weeds. He makes one more groaning attempt to see where he is and all he can understand is that he is nowhere near the road or the trees where he's familiar. But the pain from his ribs causes his arms to give way and collapse.

"Oh God. I'm hurt bad! What if I die out here? "

Mickey lies back flat on the ground, and the pain is more intense than ever. Maybe Harry and Elmer left him for dead. Maybe they dragged him away from the road and intend to come back to bury him so he'll never be found. They're probably just waiting for dark to return and finish him. He's got to get out of here, but he can't even figure where he is.

In the distance, Mickey faintly hears his name. He hears it again from a range of octaves. Ma's sent the little guys out looking for him. He tries to call out but just trying to yell hurts his ribs and jaw so badly he can't make a sound above a groan. But thank God, the voices are getting closer.

"Over here! Hey! I see him! It's Mickey. Come fast! He's over here!"

It's like sweet music when Mickey hears the excited voices coming closer. This may save his life.

"Here he is over here!"

Mickey tries to stagger to his feet, and as the kids all came running closer he knows even in the dim light he doesn't look very good.

"Eeeee!"

"Jesus, Mary, and Joseph, go get Mama!"

Colin is already running for home, "I'll go get her! I'm the fastest! Just wait here!"

These were not words of encouragement, and Mickey slumps down onto the ground again.

"He's out. Oh no, he's sort of awake. I think he's been hurt real bad."

"Mickey, can you hear me? Colin's getting Mama. She'll know what to do."

Mickey rallies all his strength, "Yeah, I hear ya. I think I can get up now."

Mickey struggles to his feet, wondering what bones are broken. He hurts really bad. Everywhere. He wonders if he'll get home and then die of his injuries. Mickey's never been this afraid and never has he been hurt this bad.

***

Later that evening Mildred O'Day wraps Mickey's ribs and cleans up his wounds as much as possible, and she stands shaking her head in sympathy at the disfigured face of her severely bruised and swollen son. "Michael, you're in rough shape. But I will say after cleanin you up, you sure look a sight better than when you got home. You've had a terrible beatin , son. As best I can tell there's no broken bones but you're gonna miss some school until ya heal a might. Then ya can go back unless ya ain't too scared or shamed to face whoever done this to ya. You know some kids will make fun of ya and that Sarge will be relishin in your misery."

Mickey tries to smile but can hardly move his mouth, "Ma, I ain't scared and I got nothin to be ashamed of. A full grown man, a Yankee soldier, ambushed me from behind. That ain't a fight. No wonder he's home. That Harry's a coward to sneak up on me like that. I could whip him in a fair face-to-face fight. I know I can fight a full grown man and I want to do it for real. Ma, I want you to sign the papers so I can join up and fight the blue bellies with Joey and…"

Mildred's mouth flies open in shock that Mickey's lying here all beat up and asking her if he can leave home and go fight. She lays the law to Mickey, "What the Sam Hill! You ungrateful brat! You think only of yerself. You'd leave this family cause you think yer the same kinda fighter as our dear Joey. Well, you ain't! You ain't joinin' the rebs or anybody else. You're stayin' right here at home where you're needed. And from the looks of you at the moment I'd say you got quite a bit of growin up to do before you start fightin growd men. You nod yer head that you understand me, or I'm gonna add another bump on that head of yourn."

"I know, Ma. I'm stuck here, and I know it. But I wanna be somebody. I know I can make you real proud, Ma…ya know, like Joe. Everybody knows who he is and I might even be better but I'm trapped here shovelin cow sh...well, I'm just workin on the farm."

Mildred isn't finished, "Thick-headed brat! You ain't joinin no army but you got business to take care of right here. You want to be a real man? Then you even the score up on this beatin you got. And Michael Sean O'Day you're gonna swear to me or get a black Irish curse, you must promise me no more talk about joinin the army and that you'll even this score...***our*** score with them lousy German Yanks."

"Yeah, okay, Ma," a dejected, sore and tired Mickey responds.

"Son, you have to think through this. You've got to think like Joey would. This is yer battle, and it's right here. You think through this real careful, even if it takes some time. You understand me, Mickey? You have to do it, or they'll never leave you, or us, alone. I must call on you this time cause I ain't got no Joey here and I ain't got no old man to fight for us or tell you what to do, so you gotta do it."

"Sure I swear it but… but...What do you want me to do?"

"Michael Sean! Saints preserve us...I just said this is where you decide to either stand up like the man you think you are or stay a little boy hangin on my apron. If you're a man, you figure out what you gotta do. But this family depends on you. Just remember that. You have to be smart about it. You could be stupid and go marchin over to that Hoenisch farm and shoot them boys, but if you do, you'll get hung, and we'd probably get burned out. Truth is, I ain't got the answer. So you think on it. I'm just scared if a bunch of Union soldiers comes through here it's no-counts like that German Hoenisch bunch that'd put them Union guys up to strippin us down to nothin and who knows what they'd do. They might burn us out completely, and I don't even want to imagine what they might do to me and your sisters."

For the next ten days, Mickey stays home from school and slowly recuperates as he tries to keep up with his chores. He wrestles with what to do about the Hoenisches. Mickey pictures himself sneaking up behind Harry and stabbing him, but that won't end it, and besides Mickey's Ma says if anybody suspects Mickey he'll likely get hung. Nope, he has to think and plan something carefully. This is bigger than Mickey popping Elmer in the nose, and it's even bigger than that rotten Harry beating Mickey with a cane. This is about family honor, Irish honor, Mickey's honor and a blow for the rebels.

Mickey feels challenged in a new and different way. He whispers to himself, "I'll be dern. I feel like a hornet in a nest by myself. Now that my nest is attacked, what the heck can I do? I'm not much of a threat, am I? Well, Ma's right. I gotta figure this out. What will a real tough guy do? What does a hero do in this situation?"

CHAPTER 3

REVENGE

A week after his beating by Harry Hoenisch and the berating by his ma, Mickey is certain everyone in his house is asleep, so he sneaks out and walks slowly along the dirt road in front of their place. He walks along trying to figure out a solution about what his ma said to him. He knows she has a mean streak and a vengeful side to her, but he's never had her make him swear he'd get even with somebody. Mickey wonders if she ever did that to Joe. Mickey smiles. Yep. He's certain Joe's character was forged by a few swearings from the invincible Ma. There are lots of ways to get even with somebody, but Mickey believes his ma is talking about doing something at a different level. He's to take care of the Hoenisch problem so that name need never be mentioned around the O'Day house.

But what should he do? What can he do? If he does anything too crazy, he'll get caught, and the frenzy of union sympathizers will hang him just to teach everybody a lesson. Some lesson! Mickey walks, heading for no particular place, but he changes his course and clammers over a fence by the road and begins to cut across the field with a little more purposeful gait. The very least he can do is sneak up close to the Hoenisch farm and take a look around. Maybe it will give him some ideas, and for sure it will let him know if he can get past their dogs and the guineas in the trees beside the Hoenisch house. Darn guineas are the undisputed champion alarm sentries any farm can have.

Mickey figures it must be midnight by now so probably all the Hoenisches are in bed. He lays down on a little knoll in the pasture and lets his eyes adjust to the dark house. All quiet and dark. But how close can he get before the guineas and the dogs offer their welcome?

Mickey sneaks as quietly as he can, still at least a hundred yards from the front porch and the guineas begin to squawk. Then the dogs begin to grumble and bark aroused from what they hoped would be a quiet night. Mickey turns tail and runs. Occasionally he looks back over his shoulder, but he never notices a light anywhere about the house. Finally, Mickey is back to the road, and he returns home as puzzled as when he sneaked out earlier.

A couple more days pass and Mickey sneaks out of the house again and with a little more determination heads directly toward the Hoenisch farm. He's got to get some ideas about what to do. This may not be a good night to get very close because he can hear the dogs barking from a distance. His curiosity is peaked, so he continues to walk toward the farm but as Mickey comes over a little rise toward the back of the farm buildings he can see the Hoenisch house is lit up like they're having a festival. Dogs are barking, Guineas are screeching. What in the world is going on?

Mickey freezes in place as he senses movement close to him. He ducks behind a feed trough and listens for any sound. He quickly sees the source of the sound near him. A man! Maybe a soldier! What's he doing out here at night? Union or Rebel?

Then Mickey's eyes adjust to see more men, and like music to his ears, the soldier speaks to a small group of men,"Oh my Irish boys of the sod it's a bleak night for our bellies. These are good folks here.   A fine family of the gray with only a few cows and our growlin stomachs that could eat em all. We'll take no more than one cow and let these folks be along with our humble thanks. We was badly misinformed. Badger won't be happy about this."

These have to be rebel soldiers and Mickey knows what he must do. "Pssst! Pssst!"

One soldier quickly points his rifle and bayonet in Mickey's direction as Mickey stands less than ten feet away with his hands raised in surrender.

"You little shit. Where the hell'd you come from? You wanna get your ass shot off? C'mere hands up, mouth shut."

Mickey does as he's told.

The soldier grabs a lantern and holds it close to Mickey's face and then continues, "What the hell'd you do? Sneak outta the house when we got here? What's yer name, kid?"

"I'm Mickey O'Day, and I heard you say boys of the sod. Some of you must be Irish I bet, and that'd be friends to my family."

"What the hell you talkin about, kid? These folks ain't Irish so where the hell did they get you? We already know from your crippled brother that you all are fine gray supporters, so you don't need to be out here sneakin around in the dark. And that red hair of yours glows pure Irish even in this light. What'd they do? Adopt ya?"

Mickey doesn't have a real plan, but he has to improvise quickly, "You have to listen to me. I'm not any part of this family. I live down the way. My brother, Joe O'Day, is a Corporal in the CSA. These are lyin Germans, all Yankees, and that crippled guy is a Union soldier. He's just mendin that leg, then he's goin back. He's the worst. These people are lying Bluecoats through and through. If you guys don't deal with em tonight, they'll get the rest of us hung, and next time ya come through here, there may not be anything but trouble for ya. I hope ya strip em to nothing. If I hadn't a seen ya I was gonna kill em and burn em out myself. Tomorrow I'm plannin on runnin from home and joinin up to serve as a soldier with my brother Joe. I mean Corporal Joe O'Day."

"Well, well. Ain't you the leprechaun bringin us the pot a' gold tonight. Listen to me. You wait here, and I'm gonna get my Sergeant. You'll talk to him? Right?"

"I'd be proud. I mean yessir. Can he enlist me tonight? I'm ready to join, and I want to fight with my brother."

"First of all, I ain't no sir. I'm better'n any sir. I'm Corporal Jack Tolliver, grunt soldier for President Jefferson Davis of this Confederate States of America. I'm purely a ground-pounder but I can fight, and I've got a few Blue ears to give my kids when I get back to my little place on the Tallapoosa in Alabam. And you are Private-to-be…? Name, boy. What's your name?"

"Yes, sir. I mean Yes, I'm Private-to-be Michael Sean O'Day but my battle name will be Mickey O'Day partner to Corporal Joseph John O'Day."

"Listen, kid, don't be throwin a name around like Joe O'Day. We all know him, and if you really his kin, the Sarge will know real quick. I like you, kid. Here, you stay right here and don't make no noise whilst I go get the Sergeant. Just so you know, Mickey O'Day, I believe ya."

"I'll be here standin my ground sir…I mean standin my ground."

Tolliver hurries from shadow to shadow making his way to where Mickey can see there are several men standing. From the couple hundred feet away and in the lanterns on the porch, Mickey sees the Hoenisches all hurrying to and fro bowing and scraping trying to continue the charade that these rebel soldiers are on a friendly property.

Soon Mickey sees Tolliver and another man making their way toward Mickey again hurrying from shadow to shadow as best they can. Mickey loses sight of them for a moment, and he's looking in the direction he last saw the two.

Suddenly a heavy hand on Mickey's shoulder from behind and Mickey is spun around to see a bearded face just inches away from his.

"Keep your voice down but answer me straight, kid. What's your name?"

In a quiet voice just above a whisper and looking straight into the bearded man's eyes, "Yes, Sir. I'm Mickey...er... uh, Michael Sean O'Day and I'll tell you everything I know…and you can be sure it'll be the truth so help me Jesus, Mary, and Joseph."

"So you claim to be the kid brother of Joe O'Day of the Badger Unit?"

"Yes, sir. Corporal Joe O'Day is my brother, and I'm proud to tell ya. But I never heard of that unit you said. He's in a special group of fighters cause he's the best fighter around these parts."

The sergeant grins a big toothy grin, "Well, kid. I don't doubt you. And you are correct about his unit. He's officially in the Company B of Special Operations Regiment, and I'm Sergeant Casey, also of Company B, and we're called the Badger Unit. So, I happen to know Joe personally, and I believe you're his brother cause there likely ain't anybody but O'Days with that red hair and freckles like you're a wearin. Now tell me exactly what you know about these people on this farm."

"Germans. Yankees. Hoenisch is their name. The Mr and Mrs. and the two sons, Elmer, about my age, and Harry. Harry was in the war, but he got shot up fightin for the Blues. That's why he's limping around with that cane. These are not good people. The boys are weasels. I beat Elmer in a fair fight last week and then his older brother Harry sneaked up on me the next day and nearly killed me with that cane of his. My Ma made me swear

I'd get even but she told me not to be stupid about it, or I'd get hung. I came over here just to try and think through it all and then here you are...and I …"

"That's enough, kid. Be quiet for a minute and let me think. C'mere, Jack."

The two soldiers walk about ten paces from Mickey and speak so quietly Mickey can't catch a single word. Soon they come back to Mickey, and the sergeant puts his hand on Mickey's shoulder and gives it a squeeze.

"Listen to me carefully, Mickey. Jack tells me you're ready to run away tonight and join up. Is that right?"

"Yes, Sir. I'm ready."

"First it's very important you not run away and try to join tonight. Not if you want in the real fightin. If you show up someplace to enlist right now, they'll put you in some hospital or at a prison camp just doin shit jobs...makin bandages, dumpin thunder mugs, moppin floors. Nope, if you really want to join to fight you have to promise me you'll wait. During the next few weeks we'll get word to you of exactly what to do. Don't tell nobody. Not yer Ma, not nobody. Got it? When my boys and I get back, my commander, Major Breault will get it all set up. You may get signed up originally as some sort of special courier or somethin just to make sure it can all get done as a legal enlistment. Once you're in all that will be changed so, don't worry about the first steps. I'm gonna tell them you're close to bein eighteen years old and if my major approves of all this, he can fix it so you won't have to prove nothing to nobody. That's why you have to wait until this gets set up. You understand?"

"Yes, sir…but…"

Sergeant pokes his index finger hard into Mickey's chest, "Yes but? Don't give me no shit when I tell you something. You keep your yezbuts to yourself. Yer only answers to me is yes Sergeant. Got that straight?"

Mickey nods his approval.

"Okay, Mickey. I want you to go on home now and don't say nothing about meeting me or the fact that any Rebs were here tonight. You confirmed what we'd been told originally about this farm. We were originally told these people are suspected of supporting Yankee spies. But I swear they was about as convincin actors as they could be. Had us convinced we had it all wrong. We aren't often fooled. Even had a reb uniform that the wounded guy said was his and just waiting to go back. They've been doing more than just talkin support for the Yanks. We're gonna put a little more persuasive pressure on these scoundrels. We'll get em to admit what they've been doing. Then we'll clean this place out tonight and leave behind stuff so's people will think it was a bunch of flea-bitten Yankee soldiers who got drunk and did what we're gonna do. You do not know nothin about this. Got it? I'm trustin you cause of Joe, and you're a solid kid. Your ma is gonna hear about this, and she may even ask you if you know anything. Your answer is you know nothing but you look deep into your Ma's eyes so's she knows you took care of your promise to her. But you say nothing, you don't even nod as if you know. You only stare into your Ma's eyes. She'll know. Look here, Mickey. You screw this up and you'll be liable to get hung and could be something worse would happen to your family. Got it?"

"Yes I do, and I'll do exactly as you say and wait for instructions." Mickey salutes the Sergeant. Standing there holding that salute, no one else but Mickey can see it but suddenly in his mind is an image of Mickey in a spotless Confederate Army uniform, shiny black leather riding boots, a sword at his side…what some day will be this Mickey O'Day in reality.

"Damn, kid. I can't wait to see Joe. He'll bust his buttons knowin what a trooper you already are. Now. Skedaddle. We got some nasty business to tend to with this lying bunch of fokkin Yank-lovers."

Mickey takes a few steps toward home, and then he begins a slow trot. His heart is pounding. What sort of rebel unit is that word he called them? Beaver? Badger? Why would a small group of soldiers be sent out this way and end up at this farm? But anyhow it sounds like on Mickey's word the Hoenisches are going to get beat up and robbed and maybe burned out. Mickey wishes they'd hang Harry. But what good will it do to leave stuff around like a bunch of Yankees did it? The Hoenisches will tell everybody what happened. Mickey stops running and turns in the general direction of the Hoenisch farm. Suddenly he knows the answer to his own question. The Hoenisches aren't going to be around to tell anybody anything. This will change Cornwall forever.

Mickey stops and sits in the grass. This is almost like killing those people himself. What if he was a soldier right now on some other farm and the Sergeant ordered him to murder the family, steal everything, and then burn it to the ground. Could he really do that? Could he use a gun, a sword, light a fire?

Mickey stands up and comes to attention out in the middle of the grassy field. He turns his body toward the Hoenisch farm and salutes into the night, "Sergeant Casey, thanks to you and my brother Joe, tonight I became a soldier, and I will live up to every order you gave me to follow. And in the future, I am willing and able to fire the first bullet, slash the first Yankee throat with a sword and light the first blaze. I am an O'Day!"

Mickey goes home, sneaks into the house past the vigilant but less-than-caring dogs. As he undresses for bed his shoes are set in a straight line beside the bed, his threadbare pants and flannel shirt are folded and put neatly on the foot of the bed. This is a turning point in the life of young Michael Sean O'Day.

CHAPTER 4

SORTING OUT LIFE

Morning comes early for Mickey, and he is genuinely tired from the excitement of the previous night. A few weeks and he can join. Maybe even sooner. But he must follow the instructions explicitly. But how will he get word of what to do? As Mickey enters the kitchen area to pick up his dinner bucket for school, he notices Ma's attention is glued to something outside as she stares out the window.

"You okay, Ma?"

Mickey's ma turns to him, "Can't say for sure but it looks like black smoke coming from either the Mosier or Hoenisch place. Probably somebody's got a fire in a hay barn or something."

Mickey doesn't even make eye contact with his ma. He just scrunches his shoulders in a silent response that indicates he has no idea and really doesn't care. "See ya this afternoon, Ma."

"Michael O'Day, please try to come home in one piece and without half your bones popped,"

"I'm fine, Ma. I ain't lookin for no trouble. But seems there's always somebody lookin to do dirt to somebody else. Like that School-Marm Barrows." Mickey twists his face, "The Sarge. He's just plain mean, and it wouldn't surprise me if he and Harry Hoenisch were big buddies…being yellow-bellied Yanks and all."

“Well, you do your best to stay outta trouble, but one of these days you gotta take care of that promise you made to me about that Hoenisch Yank.”

“Yeah, Ma. See ya,”

On the way to school, Mickey and his brothers and sisters take their time talking and making slow progress, so they arrive at school just in time for the first bell of the morning. Sarge Barrows stands on the front steps ringing the handbell in all directions, his oak pointer leans against the door facing. With about half the students inside the school and the rest hurrying across the front yard of the school, attention swings suddenly to a man on horseback at full gallop heading for the schoolhouse.

As he nears the front yard, he brings the horse up smartly and jumps off, “Sarge! Sarge! I need to see ya before you get started.”

Sarge sets the bell down on the step, picks up his pointer and makes a fast walk toward the horseman, “What the hell, Nicolas Koch! Where’s the fire, man?”

By now all eyes are on the two men, and Sarge listens intently and shakes his head as if in disbelief. About the only thing Mickey makes out is the name, Wilfred. That’s Mr. Hoenisch’s first name, the dirty old German Yankee. Sergeant Casey and Jack Tolliver’s guys probably set their barn on fire and took all the animals. But deep inside Mickey’s stomach feels fluttery. He doesn’t feel fluttery from fright or queasy from guilt, just fluttery excited to think about what he guesses may have happened to the Hoenisches. This is war.

Sarge herds the remaining gawkers into the classroom, and it's plain as day to see that he's upset. Instead of whacking his pointer on the schoolmaster's desk or the desk of an unfortunate, inattentive student, he taps his pointer lightly on the blackboard, "I need your attention. Quiet, please. Class come to order."

It's so unusual for Sarge to be talking in a quiet voice the class is immediately silent, looking at him.

"Most of you saw Nicolas Koch ride up a few minutes ago with some news. We are going to do something totally different today, and I need for you to listen carefully. First of all, I want all the girls in this room to go outside for a few minutes. I want you to sit on the front steps or stand right next to them. I'm going to talk to the boys alone. Now girls listen to me. No going to the toilet or playing in the yard. You must sit by the steps. If you see anyone approaching the school, you are to open the door and tell me. Now I won't keep the boys long so just wait for them to come out. Then we'll all gather back in here, and I'll give you further instructions. Okay, young ladies, outside with you and stay by the front door. Go ahead now."

There are murmuring and whispers as the girls exit outside. Sarge stands by the door until the last girl is outside and then he slowly walks back to the front. All eyes are on Sarge.

"Listen to me boys and listen well so you can tell your folks at home about this. There's not a good way to put this, but last night the entire Hoenisch family was murdered, robbed and burnt out of house and buildings. Everything's gone at the Hoenisch place. Everything.

The girls could have been told but here's the details as we know them right now. It looks like a group of army renegades did this. Who knows? Deserters? Escapees from military prison? They may have been in Yankee uniforms, but they don't represent the Union Army, and I'm sure the army will catch up to them. But in the meantime, we don't know exactly who they are or worse, where they are. So whatever men the Sheriff can round up are gonna come to the school and ride or walk with you to be sure everyone gets home safely. Then you need to make sure your Pa and Ma know about this or Ma, if your Pa's gone, because if they're still around here, they might do something bad again tonight."

A hand shoots up into the air waving to get Sarge's attention.

"Yes. Question?"

"Yes, Sir. Should we come back to school tomorrow? I mean will it be safe tomorrow?

"Well, since this is Thursday, I declare there will be no school tomorrow, but unless you hear different, you come back on time on Monday morning. You understand?"

Everyone smiles, scoots around in the seats and nods affirmatively.

Another boy calls out to Sarge, "Do you mean Elmer was killed, too?"

"Yes. That's why I said the entire family. More curiosity about the details. Okay, then…you're boys and some of you want to already be men. Part of bein a man is knowing reality, and sooner or later you're gonna know the world isn't always a pretty sight. So I'm gonna tell you what I was told. The four members of the Hoenisch family were beaten and then hung in the big walnut tree in front of their house. There's not a stitch on any of them, and that could mean there was unspeakable things that took place. Don't know nothing about that as of now. Harry, the wounded war hero, was beaten so bad with his own cane his own mama wouldn't have recognized him if she was still alive, which she isn't…God rest her soul. Now, that's all I know, and so now you know. Make you feel all grown up does it? Make ya feel sick to your stomach? Well, it ought to. Ya know, some of you boys should be so angry from this you should talk your folks into letting you enlist. The Hoenisches were a fine family and supporters of this United States, I wish I could tell you it was rebs that killed those folks but it looks like it was a god-damned bunch of our very own…deserters… misfits…runners. When they do get caught, they'll be shot or hung just as if they had been rebs. Either hanging or shooting is too good for these lowlifes. Okay. Now any more questions?"

The boys all look down at their desks. Mickey was pretty sure last night on the way home he knew what was going to happen but he had no idea how brutal it would turn out to be. Mickey reinforces in his young mind that he needs to do exactly as he was told and he is further galvanized into the acceptance of his willingness to be a Confederate soldier no matter what he may be called upon to do.

The girls are asked to re-enter the school, and for the next hour, Sarge keeps the room fairly quiet. Children who need to use the toilet are allowed to go, but three volunteer students stand between the front door of the school and the outdoor toilet dispersed far enough apart so they can sound a warning if anything out of the ordinary is noticed. A few men arrive at the school and Sarge draws a rather crude area map of Cornwall and the surrounding area so he can dispatch children with an armed escort to get home.

Mr. Jim Wilkens is assigned to take the O'Days and the Lehman's home. Jim is old, hard of hearing and can't see very well but he is on horseback and has a rifle so it's about as good as can be expected though not much more than a trifle of defense in case of trouble. Mickey thinks to himself how frightened everyone is of this so-called band of Yankee renegades when all along Mickey knows them by name and considers himself a sort-of member of the group at this moment. His job is to follow instructions and sign up as soon as he gets contacted.

When the O'Days arrive home Ma is surprised to see them and asks what happened. Mickey explains in detail what Sarge told the boys. He resists editorializing on the brutality and who deserved what. When Mickey finishes there isn't anymore said and having a day off from school is to be enjoyed.

At one point in the afternoon, Mickey walks out on the back porch where Ma is darning repairs to several waiting pairs of socks in various sizes. She pats the seat of a rocking chair next to her and indicates for Mickey to sit down and he yawns, stretches, and then sits.

"Michael, I guess that smoke I saw this morning was what was left of the Hoenisch farm. And here I thought it was just some hay or something caught fire. All of em murdered and everything burned by their very own Yankee Army. Hard to imagine why."

Mickey says nothing and continues to look at his Ma. She continues, "And I want you to know I heard you come back in the house last night. I know it was long, long after midnight. Probably closer to three. Strange you'd be out sneaking around when something like this happens. Good thing you didn't run headlong into those murderers, huh?"

Mickey says nothing but shrugs his shoulders as if he has no knowledge of any of this. Mickey's Ma stops her mending and looks Mickey in the eyes, "You involved with killin'?"

"Mickey remembers what Sergeant Casey instructed him about communicating with his Ma just by looking at her. Now Mickey knows exactly what Sergeant Casey meant. He stares almost hypnotically at his Ma.

" No idea about any of it."

The two sit and stare into each others'eyes. Then his Ma breaks the gaze, looks down and concentrates on sock repairs. "Goodness sakes but you kids can go through the heels and toes of socks faster than I can mend em."

Mickey gets up from the chair, walks to the edge of the porch, yawns, and stretches. He hitches his pants up a bit and turns slightly toward his Ma, "It feels kinda funny being out of school early today. I may as well go do the chores and be done with them. Probably best not to be outside after dark too much until they catch those Yanks."

Mickey hops down from the porch and heads toward the barn. He feels so confident and happy it's difficult for him to believe. Everybody's chasing a bunch of what they think are murdering Yanks and Mickey knows the real truth and the real people who did this good deed for the community. And the real men…the real soldiers are long gone, and soon Mickey will be gone as well.

CHAPTER 5

YES, SIR, I DO

Sunday comes way too soon for seven kids enjoying no school. Mickey's Ma has big plans for this bright Sunday. Her brood is to complete some extra chores around the house and she'll fix a special fried chicken Sunday dinner. She gets the children up from bed at the same time as if they are going to school. As they come downstairs to their usual breakfast of pork cracklins and cornmeal mush, Ma has their duties all lined up for the day. Mickey is to help his Ma plant the garden. It is nearly halfway through April, and there's not much danger of frost so all the little sprouts Mildred O'Day nursed through the winter will now go into the garden. She counts on vegetables to provide needed food for their family and then in the fall, and before it turns too cold she'll pick what's left, preserve what she can and store some in the root cellar.

Around ten or so that morning Mildred stands up and shades her eyes trying to get a better view of a lone rider coming slowly toward the house.

"Mickey, you see that guy comin up the road?"

"Sure, Ma. I see him. Who is it?"

"Of course I wouldn't know who it is, Michael Sean O'Day. But I want you to go get the shotgun and sit with it up on the porch. Don't point it or fool around with it. I simply want whoever this is to see it and state his intentions real quick. Now scoot!"

Mickey does as he's told and as he enters the house he yells at all the others to come to the kitchen. Mickey gets the shotgun out of the closet, breaks the breech, and pops a shell into the chamber. He grabs four more shells and stuffs them in his pocket. The gun feels pretty good in his hands and he feels empowered to be the appointed acting man-of-the-house, at least for a few fleeting moments. But Mickey can't help but hope to get a uniform and rifle as soon as he gets in the real army.

As the children gather and see Mickey with the gun they begin running toward the windows.

"Mickey. Where's Ma?"

What's going on, Mick?"

"You all calm down. There's one man on a horse coming up the road and Ma just wants to be a little careful. You all stay in the house until I give you instructions. Understand?"

Mickey looks at each of them, "I want to hear you say yes Sir."

All the children laugh at Mickey's assumed power. Mickey in frustration makes a motion with his hand toward them like they don't understand and then hurries out the front door and onto the porch. He sits in the rocking chair he was in yesterday talking with his Ma. The shotgun lies across his lap as he can't keep from imagining how imposing his defensive figure must be to the strange rider.

The rider's physical appearance is very clear now, and it doesn't look like much of a threat. The rider looks older and weather-beaten, but he has a really nice looking horse. He's a tall man and sits straight in the saddle with an assumed air of importance. He continues to approach with his hat removed, out of respect for Mickey's Ma. He has snow white hair and a long bushy mustache that blends into a short beard on his very tan, leathery face.

The man is smiling and talking to Ma, and though she has her back to Mickey, he senses from her reactions she's not feeling threatened. Shortly afterward the man gets down from his horse, and he begins walking with Mickey's ma toward the porch. Mickey stands up, uncertain what he should do next.

His Ma gives the closest she can muster to a smile, " Michael Sean, this here is Preacher Yount and he's passing through Cornwall on his way on down to Arkansas. True he ain't no Irish priest of the Sacred Word, but we can do with God in this house any way we can get it…particularly on a Sunday. Preacher Yount will have Sunday dinner with us, and I need for you to water and feed his horse. So put that gun back in the closet and take care of this for me."

The preacher steps forward before Mickey can return the gun inside. "And a fine young man you appear to me, Michael. I'll take this saddle off of Boaz and give him a little rest, too."

Mickey props the gun against the door facing and steps forward on the porch, "Oh I can take the saddle off, and when you get ready I can resaddle and cinch him. I'm good with horses."

With a clear and irritated voice, the preacher points at the gun, "Why would I trust my horse with some snot-nosed kid who hasn't obeyed his Ma… nor has the good sense to handle a gun safely? Tell you what, you put the gun away like your mother instructed you, and then you come back out here. ***Then*** you and I will take care of the horse together. Understand me, Boy?"

Mickey's Ma takes a step back at the preacher's gruff tone, and Mickey nods his head that he understands.

The preacher stares straight at Mickey, "Usually I get an answer when I ask a question. I don't think a nod gets the job done. Understand?"

"Yes, Sir." Mickey stands erect when he answers. He promptly picks up the shotgun and hastens into the house. With the front door standing open it's easy to hear when Mickey breaks the breech of the gun and removes the shells. He quickly reappears at the door and stands erect very close to the preacher.

"Sir, I'm ready to help you with your horse."

The preacher's eyes soften, and he looks like he's about to smile, but a smile never appears as he says in a calm, almost kind voice, "Alright, Michael, let's go together and take care of Boaz. I'm anxious to see how good you really are with horses."

Mickey jumps off the front porch and walks to the horse, and begins to loosen the reins that tie him to the water pump handle.

The preacher turns and walks to where Mickey is standing with the horse. The two of them walk toward the barn and water trough. The O'Day children are still glued to the windows watching what's been taking place. Mickey's Ma is left standing alone, so she goes up the steps into the house.

As Mickey and the preacher walk silently toward the barn, the preacher breaks the silence. "Guess I'm a little more direct than you expected of a broken down old parson."

Mickey looks up at the preacher but is reluctant to say anything, but he certainly would agree with that statement. This old man seems to be very direct and authoritarian.

The preacher continues, "Maybe my directness comes from the fact I'm not a preacher. I'm Colonel William Maxwell, Army of the Confederacy. Just keep walking with me, and I'll explain. Understand?"

Mickey stops on a dime and looks up at him, "Yes, Sir. I understand…well, Sir, sort of…well, Sir, I'm not sure I understand at all."

"Michael O'Day, I am the Deputy Commander of the Recruiting and Training Depot south of Little Rock Arkansas. I'm heading back there, and a very special unit of our soldiers got word about you, and since I had to make this trip anyhow, I made the opportunity to detour through Cornwall. I'm going to swear you in right here in this barn and give you reporting instructions. Understand?"

Mickey beams from ear to ear, "Yes Sir, Colonel, Sir. I'm ready to serve."

"Alright then. We'll step inside the barn, and I'll give you the oath of enlistment."

Mickey can hardly contain himself. He trusted Sergeant Casey that there would be contact but this really surprises him. Its only been a few days. And a full Colonel!

"Alright, Michael, we don't need to draw too much suspicion with your family by being out here in the barn too long so let me explain the enlistment papers. I'm going to read you the entire paper, and then I'm going to have you sign two copies of it. I keep one and take it with me back to my headquarters, and you keep the other one. And I wouldn't be showing it to anybody around Cornwall. But bring it with you when you travel to camp…and I'll tell you how that will happen in just a moment. Before I read this, I want to be sure you are ready, willing and able to fight. You're pretty damn young to get into the thick of the fighting, but if that's what your heart's set on, I need to hear you say it. And once we count on you as a soldier, you can't go changing your mind and running back home. That's called desertion, and it's dealt with harshly. So be sure of your intentions."

"Yes, Sir, Colonel, Sir. I'm joinin to fight and not to play no drum or anything like a kid would do. I want to be treated like a man, and I'll prove myself to be a good soldier of the Confederacy I want to fight in battle along side my big brother, Corporal Joey O'Day in the Twenty-Third Regiment of the Tennessee Volunteers."

"I know personally of your brother as I do most of the men picked to be in Major Breault's Badger Unit and your brother is a heroic credit to his regiment, Michael. Okay, then I'm going to have you swear you're eighteen years old and I'm going to swear I believe you. Let those be the only two lies either of us ever tells each other again. When you sign the papers, you'll officially be Private Michael O'Day, but you and I will keep up this Preacher Yount act for the remainder of my visit. I won't be calling you anything but Michael, and you call me nothing except Preacher Yount. No siree. No Colonel. Guard your speaking very carefully. Even with your family. Understand?"

"Yes, I understand, Preacher Yount." Mickey smiles a big smile, and the Colonel matches it and puts a hand on Mickey's shoulder as a gesture of appreciation of Mickey's quick understanding.

Colonel Maxwell continues, "Michael, you'll need to catch the southbound train out of Cornwall Station next Wednesday around noon. You'll get to Poplar Bluff early evening, and you catch the train goin West to Sulphur Springs. You'll travel through the night and get into the Springs about mid-afternoon the next day. When you get to Sulphur Springs, you get off the train and wait at the train station on the West end of the building. The West end. There will likely be some other men there as well...waitin to get picked up. We pick up new soldiers and recruits there every other day just around dark so don't go wandering off around town or you'll get left behind. The man who picks you up will not be in uniform, and his name is Beauford. Everything's different from there on. Don't think old Beauford is some old drunk. Beauford's a buffalo skinner, and he's an army all by himself. Just do whatever Beauford says. He'll take you in a wagon over to the regiment. That's where you'll get your uniform, training and be assigned to your first unit. By the way, don't ever tell your Ma or anybody else around here about me because I come through this area pretty regular on my way to and from New Madrid. If I get caught by the Yanks, and they find out who I am I get hung as a spy. Lots of information but you clear on what to do?"

"Yes. I'm clear on what to do. Wednesday can't get here soon enough."

"One other thing, Michael. As soon as I read this to you and you sign it, I hand you fifty dollars as an enlistment bounty. Do with it what you will but be careful you don't spark somebody's attention before you leave. My advice is don't spend any of it until the day you're leaving. You can always leave some with your Ma but keep enough to buy your train ticket and some food until you get to camp. The train ticket is two dollars, and four to six bits will cover any meals you want to get along the way."

Mickey is concentrating on the details, but he's very clear on what to do and when. He's not sure how to tell his Ma properly. He will figure out a way to catch that train next Wednesday and maybe he'll leave his ma a letter with some money, but he'll seal it in an envelope and have his oldest sister bring it home after school the day he leaves. No goodbyes. He'll head for school Wednesday but complain of being sick before he gets there. Then he'll give his sister the letter and go straight to the train station in plenty of time to catch the train to his first stop in Poplar Bluff.

Colonel Maxwell reads the enlistment form to Mickey. As he concludes reading, he removes his spectacles, stares at Mickey and says, "Okay, Michael you sign here on both copies, and I'll sign them."

Colonel Maxwell watches Mickey signing to be a combat soldier, and he smiles because he's signed up many men who were reported to be pretty tough, but he's seen their hands shake like a leaf as they sign the enlistment papers. Mickey's hand is steady, and he even looks up a couple of times smiling from ear to ear. Colonel Maxwell knows this is a good man, not a daredevil boy.

They take care of the horse and eventually walk back to the house where a wonderful spread of food is waiting.

"Mrs. O'Day. I swan. I've never seen God's providential bounty spread in any better fashion than this. I humbly thank you and your God-fearing family."

Ma smiles and wipes her hands nervously on her apron, "Preacher Yount, as I told you we ain't got no parish priest out here and never have. You bein a man of the cloth will just have to do for even us Irish Catholics. Maybe you can bless our house and these kids before you leave. I only wish my bunch of heathens had learned the catechism and had their confession and first communion…and Lord's sake if only they'd been to a proper confession. But a priest would have to bring dinner, supper and a bedroll to the confessional to listen to the list of blackguard sins this bunch has been piling up. "

"It will be an honor for me to bless your house and family and it will be glory to God. And Mrs. O'Day, I am Protestant, but I carry the necessaries for communion if you'd be comfortable with it. We'd be bending more of your beliefs than mine, so it's whatever you're comfortable with doing or not doing."

Mildred O'Day looking a bit surprised and with a half smile on her face bursts into tears, "Oh Preacher, you are an angel. Truly an angel sent to my house. Let's eat while everything is hot, but the torture in my life can only be erased by my confession and communion." She lifts her apron over her head without untying it and wipes her eyes with it as she sits at the table.

Mickey admires Colonel Maxwell for his acting skills and he thinks it must be entertaining to pretend you're someone you're not and still be doing your job as a soldier. He's so proud he only wishes he could tell everyone at the table about his exciting future. His heart is about to jump out of his body! But he's been instructed, and he is bound and determined to live up to his responsibilities.

After they eat, the colonel gathers his communion supplies from his saddlebags and prepares an altar and serves communion. He bids everyone farewell, shakes hands with Mickey, looking him square in the eyes and then mounts Boaz and rides slowly out of sight.

CHAPTER 6

TIME TO MEET THE ARMY

Finally! Wednesday arrives. Daybreak sheds its light over the quiet little farm. Mickey has been awake most of the night rehearsing every detail so he's ready for this day. He carefully re-counts the money for his ma and the money he'll take. He seals the envelope with the money and the letter to his ma. Mickey makes no apologies in the letter but reasserts his insatiable desire to prove himself as a man who will make his ma and family proud. Though he misspells the word "legend", Mickey states his intention to ride back home one day with everyone knowing who he is and knowing his bravery and heroics as a soldier. The envelope is inside Mickey's pocket, and he looks around his room feeling excitement about leaving. Even Mickey is surprised that he feels no sadness or nostalgia of happy times past.

Later, as Mickey, his brothers and his sisters get in sight of the schoolyard, Mickey feigns pain and groans out loud. Ailbe looks over at Mickey, "Hey, what's wrong?"

Mickey responds with a pained look, "I don't feel so good. Probably nothin to worry about. But if I get to feelin bad, I may have to go on home early. If that happens one or two of you just tell Sarge, I was feelin sick on the way to school. He won't care. He'll probably be happy imagining me in pain."

That a good enough explanation for the O'Day clan, and they silently turn to continue their march toward a stimulating day of education.

At first recess, Mickey walks over to Aileen and matter-of-factly says, "Listen, Aileen, I know I can trust you to do exactly what I say. I'm gonna leave school when everybody goes in after recess. You tell Sarge I'm sick. Okay? Ailbe will say the same."

"Oh Mickey, I hope it don't hurt too bad. And sure I'll tell Sarge…and we'll be fine to get home after school."

"Okay, now this is real important. You give this envelope to Ma when you get home. Don't show the envelope to nobody. Not Sarge, not any of our schoolmates, not any of our brothers and sisters. It goes only to Ma. You understand?"

"Sure, I understand what you're sayin, but I don't understand. If you're sick why aren't ya goin home? Where you goin or what you gonna do this afternoon?"

"Aileen. I'm not really sick but I'm trustin you to do this exactly like I'm tellin you. And no more questions. Give this only to Ma, and that's it. I know I can trust you. Right?"

"Of course ya can."

Aileen takes the envelope and tucks it in a pocket of her long skirt.

Mickey innocently makes his way to the edge of the school grounds, and when Sarge sticks one arm out of the door and rings the bell, the rest of the students head noisily for the door and Mickey steps over the low fence and heads down the road. He looks back a couple of times, but no one appears around the school. Surely by now, Aileen has told Sarge, and that's that. Time for the Michael Sean O'Day adventure to begin.

CHAPTER 7

WELCOME TO THE ARMY

Mickey cuts through a field and gets to the train tracks. He heads down the familiar tracks and makes his way cross the trestle over Castor River. He recalls all the times crossing the trestle kids listened carefully for any trains. Being caught on the trestle meant a dive into the river some seventy-five feet below. Mickey recalls the time he and another boy climbed on top of the iron beams of the trestle and let the train pass beneath them. What a mistake. The hot cinders from the train's coal-fired engine burned them badly and they felt lucky to be alive. Another time they deliberately waited for a train and then showed off by diving into the deep pool of the river beneath the bridge. Once of that was enough as well because that height bruised Mickey's body and felt like his shoulders were dislocated after hitting the water. Mickey stands a little taller as he walks, leaving behind childhood memories and ready, oh so ready, in another twenty-five yards or so to be at his first destination, the Cornwall Train Station.

The wooden building is in bad need of repair but he's only been inside twice before when Ma took all the kids to Sikeston to visit some distant relative of his pa. The sign over the entrance in all capital letters "CORNWALL" is like a marquee welcoming Mickey to building his personal legend.

Mickey pauses for a moment outside the train station, takes a breath and tries to appear tall and confident as he approaches the ticket window. No matter how straight he stands or how he tries to appear bigger, he knows he's simply not the imposing stature of a hero. Not yet.

Inside the ticket window is the familiar face of Mr. Bert Phillips. Mickey knows his face but doubts if Mr. Phillips knows him.

"Well, howdy do, young man. Say, ain't you Joe's little brother?

"Yessir. Michael."

"Sure. Thought I recognized you. What can I help you with?"

I need a ticket to Popular Bluff."

"Sure. Goin on a trip by yerself? What ya going there for?"

"Oh, Ma's sister is poorly and she wants me to help her out til she gets a bit better."

"OH, sorry to hear that. That will be four bits for the ticket. Train should be here in about fifteen minutes so you ain't got long to wait."

"Thanks, Mr. Phillips. I'll just wait outside on the platform."

Mickey gets his ticket and finds a spot to sit on a platform bench. Mr. Phillips never suspected a thing. Looks like it's just Mickey and three mailbags waiting for the southbound train.

His bravery begins to unravel as he sits. He squirms as he can't control his sudden fear. He's leaving his Ma and family to fend for themselves. No matter how tall he tries to stretch himself or puff out his chest, he looks like a sixteen-year-old kid. Maybe he looks even more like a fourteen-year-old. What if he gets to the fort and they take one look at him, laugh and send him home? The army is what he's wanted. What he's dreamed about. Now he's got it.

If the wait for the train had been a long time who knows what second thoughts Mickey may have had. But the train is on time and Mickey dutifully steps aboard and finds a seat.

Mickey gets off the train in Poplar Bluff and approaches the station clerk, "Sir, maybe you can help me... I need a ticket to get to Sulphur Springs."

The clerk looks rather disagreeably at Mickey and then smiles and winks, "Ticket to Sulphur Springs, huh? I'll bet you're joinin up with the Rebs. Well, ya may not be the biggest recruit I've seen, but yep, I guess you got what ya need to help the cause. Just sit on that bench, and I'll tell ya when it's time to leave. Don't worry from here. After you get off at the Springs they'll send somebody to take ya the rest of the way. You'll get to the fort alright. And God bless ya, Son. "

As promised, the clerk comes out about a half hour before the train is due to come and he brings Mickey a couple slices of bread, a thick piece of smoked ham and a tin cup of water. He can't help but notice the clerk's dirty hands and black fingernails but the sandwich and water taste just fine. He figures he'd better get used to a little rougher way of existing. Nobody talks about frills or clean fingernails when they talk about army life.

From here on there won't be food like his ma would be fixing for him.

Right on time, the train going West comes into the station, the clerk follows Mickey on board and with obvious pride, tells the conductor and those within earshot that he is a Confederate Army recruit. Some of the passengers smile and give a nod of encouragement. The slight gestures of respect scratch Mickey's obsession for self-worth. Now he suddenly feels great!

The train clackity clacks and rocks from side to side with the occasional stops at small towns. It is a long, sleepless night on the train and there are several little stops along the way. But after each stop the train rattles west. Finally in the early afternoon the conductor announces they are approaching the Sulphur Springs Station.

Mickey hops off the train. Somehow, the lack of rest, the new area, the strangers' encouragement cause Mickey to feel a little woozy. If he were older and knew alcohol's effect he'd have said it was intoxicating, but at this point, the virginal soldier simply feels woozy. Following the Colonel's directions, Mickey goes to the west end of the Sulphur Springs Station building. There are two men sitting on the ground leaning against the building. One is mindlessly whittling with a pocket knife and the other with a large cloth bag for a pillow, hat pulled down over his face, is apparently asleep. Mickey says nothing but sits off to one side of the two men.

The man whittling looks over at Mickey, spits some tobacco juice and wipes across his mouth with his shirt sleeve before he speaks," Kid, I think you got the wrong end of the building here or is General Lee takin kids direct from their sugar tit to be soldiers?"

Mickey hears every word, and his heart beats fast. He doesn't want to start off on the wrong foot but this guy seems to be looking for trouble, and Mickey wants none of it. So Mickey just turns his head and ignores the comment.

The man stops whittling and looks at Mickey, "Hey, Kid. Hard of hearin?"

The other man with the hat over his face slowly lifts his hat, looks at Mickey and then looks at the other man, "Look here. My name's David. David Mitchell. I'm from just outside Ironton, Missouri to join up. Don't know your name or this young man's name but seems to me you got no call pickin at either one of us. We might all wind up standing next to each other one day with our muskets looking at a line of blue. Let's get along for now."

Mickey speaks up, " My name's Mickey O'Day. I'm from a little town called Cornwall up by Fredericktown, Missouri. I'm eighteen, and I'm joining to fight. The only enemies I got are the yellow-bellied Yanks. I know I look young and I ain't gonna brag, but I'm a pretty darn good fighter. My brother, Joe's a really good fighter, and he's a corporal in the Twenty-Third over in Tennessee."

The man who had stirred things initially, spits, wipes his mouth and smiles, "Boys, this big yapper on the front of my ugly face is owned by James Boyle. My little no-count farm over by Cairo, Illinois got burned out by the

Yankees, and so I got a score to settle. I consider myself a pretty good fighter, too, Mickey, and I hate to admit it, but I'm nervous as a cat til we get uniforms, guns and turned loose with the army. Meant no trouble to ya son."

The three of them smile and sit silently.

The early evening turns to the black of night and around ten o'clock the three spot a wagon pulled by two mules, slowly rounding the end of the train station where it draws to a stop right next to them.

There's only one flickering gas light close to the wagon, but it's easy to tell that Colonel Maxwell-Preacher Yount did not over embellish the driver's demeanor. Without a word, he jumps from the wagon, unbuttons his overalls, digs a bit for his privates and then begins a hearty urine stream facing directly toward the three men sitting by the wagon. They all jump to their feet to stay out of a possible soaking. After a prolonged shaking off his member he spits a mighty wad of tobacco juice onto the wall and then buttons his overall straps.

Mickey is fascinated by what he can see of the driver's appearance. He's comical in some ways, and yet there's an air of danger that emanates from him. He's so skinny that the straps of his overalls hang on his bony shirtless shoulders. The rest of the body of this little man has lots of freedom inside the pants. His gray or dirty blonde hair makes a near perfect circle like a wreath around his head and face. His eyes are deep set, and his pointy nose accentuates his eyebrows, so it's like he's perpetually angry. His mouth is nowhere to be seen in all the bushy beard and hair.

And then the tiny mouth in all that hair speaks, “Boys, I’m Beauford, and I don’t stand on no ceremony. Maybe you noticed. I ain’t got no last name. Just Beauford. I ain’t got no interesting stuff to talk about, and I really ain’t interested in anything you got to say, so we’ll just stick to business. I’m under contract with these Confederate States of America to meet you here and take ya to the camp. I spose that’s what you’re here for. Right? And if’n you’re afraid of the dark, don’t worry. Jist don’t whine out loud cause that bothers my mules. I ain’t never lost a man on these dark roads.”

All three nod and begin moving toward the wagon. David throws his bag in the back of the wagon and grabs hold of a side-stake to pull himself up.

Beauford jumps straight at David. “Hold the fuck on! What do ya think yer doin? You don’t get in my wagon until you give me the secret password. All of youse, one at a time come forward and whisper it to me. If it’s wrong, I’ll figure you’re a Yank spy, and maybe I’ll just slice yer ass like a Christmas goose. And Boys, I ‘m pretty damn good with my sling blade.”

From what appears to be a long pocket down the side of one leg of his overalls Beauford pulls a knife with a blade about eighteen inches long. He stabs and sticks it in the side of the wagon. He pauses and looks at the three, spits some tobacco and picks up a shotgun from the wagon seat, “What the hell! Ain’t none of ya comin forward or sayin a thing?”

James nervously wipes his mouth with his sleeve, “Now hold on here...something ain’t right...I for one ain't never got no password.”

Beauford stares at James and lifts the shotgun in a threatening manner. The three recruits are frozen in place and then just as quick, Beauford laughs and slaps his leg several times, “That’s cause there ain’t no password. I’m justa cuffin yer carrots.”

He laughs some more and slaps his leg as he really seems to enjoy what he just did.“Okay. C’mon. Climb aboard. Shit, boys, that’s the only joke I know, and nobody but me ever laughs at it. Aint none of ya wet yerself did ya?”

The three don’t answer but look at each other and shake their heads showing disbelief. They are quickly in the wagon, and Beauford turns the mules and starts the journey.

Drifting in and out of sleep, hearing the steady slow hoofbeats, the night seems like it will last forever. Daylight finally breaks, and Beauford shifts around on his seat, “Rise and shine, ladies. We should get to the fort in about an hour.”

As the wagon arrives at Camp Whitespring, the three new soldiers are silent, staring at the guard house and gate. The wagon approaches, the sentry emerges from the gatehouse and stands with his rifle across his chest. Beauford pulls to a stop. The sentry walks around the wagon with his rifle, staring at the three recruits, his face of grim superiority. It’s not clear to any of them what he is inspecting, but he completes his circle of the wagon, winks at Beauford and unceremoniously waves them through without so much as a single word between driver and sentry. After entering the gate, the gravel road looks as if it’s freshly raked and the sound of the wagon's wheels crunch the roadway as if intruding on someone's hard work. The drive makes a circle around the grassy centerpiece with a spectacular flagpole in the center and a huge confederate flag. On the back side of the circle is a white colonial building with columns and two huge doors. Though it is early morning, soldiers are streaming in and out of the building. That must be the headquarters. Mickey is impressed with the spit and polish of the entrance. He wonders if the big building will be their first stop to get checked in to become real soldiers. He will sure be glad to get his uniform, sword, and rifle. Then he'll know he's a real live soldier and then he'll feel qualified to meet Joe as brothers in arms.

The wagon goes laboriously around the circle, passes by the big building and keeps going on the gravel road to the left of the entry. The gravel on this section of road doesn't look well-maintained like the entry and people walking stir up dust as they walk. In the distance, Mickey sees long lines of dark tents, hundreds of them, maybe thousands. The complex of tents seems to go on and on. Many of the soldiers must still be asleep, but there's still a lot of activity and particularly men pausing, looking at the wagon and smiling. Some laugh to one another as if the three recruits are the day's entertainment.

There doesn't appear to be any more big buildings except the one at the entrance. Just an endless sea of brown, water-stained, bedraggled canvas tents. The wagon makes a right turn and stops by a long tent with all four sides exposed to the outside. There are people in line, and it looks to Mickey as if this is where they will probably get uniforms. Thank goodness, Mickey thinks to himself.

Beauford turns slightly toward the three who almost appear to be cowering in the wagon as if looking for Beauford to rescue them. Beauford spits tobacco and says, "Now just keep your seats, Lads. The good Sarge, Sergeant Boskins, should come for ya in a minute or two. Let's us hope for the good Sarge cause if he's too busy he'll send Corporal Grounds and he's a downright mean sonuvabitch. Somethin wrong with that boy...just mean. Well, anyhow, we'll hope the Sarge, Old Boskins comes for ya."

Mickey stirs around a bit in the back of the wagon trying to get more comfortable if that's even possible and as he diverts his attention to his comfort he hears Beauford in a sort of whisper, "Drat the luck boys. It ain't Boskins for ya. It's Corporal Grounds. Oh well. Good luck to ya anyhow. Ya might want to get out and say howdy afore he clouds up and rains on ya. "

Mickey looks up, and there's Corporal Grounds several feet away, focused on the men in the wagon, and he doesn't appear to need too much introduction after what Beauford said. Mickey once saw a picture of a bear standing erect, and this man before him merely has a shorter snout. He's enormous at well over six feet, and there's lots of meat on his big bones. It's difficult to see his mouth because of the very black, bushy mustache that stands out against his fiery red face. His dark red nose is big and looks to be pockmarked. His black hair sticks out and seems very shaggy for a soldier, and that's just the hair that can be seen coming from under what was once his grey cap. The cap is greasy and sweat-stained and his uniform wrinkled and dirty. But the most descriptive part of this giant is his unpleasant facial expression. It's like somebody just made him so angry he's about to spit.

"Well, I guess you little girls are waiting for me to invite ya out of that wagon so okay…" Corporal Grounds takes an aggressive step forward so he's about a foot or so from Mickey's face and he screams in his booming voice, spittle showering all three, "***Get yer fuckin asses outta that wagon! Stand at attention here in fronta me***!"

All three jump from the wagon and stand still, glancing around at each other and back at the huge man in front of them, waiting for what's next.

Corporal Grounds looks like he wants to punch someone or something, and though he lowers his voice it is so sarcastic, sharp and penetrating Mickey at least thinks one of the three is going to get clobbered by this guy.

Grounds tone of voice seeths as he snarls, "Let me not forget my manners. Congratulations, Gentlemen. You are now the property of the Confederate States Army for the next twelve months. From now on you listen to me like I'm your momma but I got at least one difference. Unlike yer mama, I don't love ya little darlins. In fact, I don't even like ya til ya prove yer worth a shit. When I tell ya to move, you're gonna get your crap outta that wagon, get your enlistment papers and get back over here in front of me...at attention. Attention means standing straight, hands at sides, feet together, and no looking around. Your eyeballs better be in a cage when I tell ya to be at attention. Now let's see if you three can handle all those really hard instructions. ***Move***!"

Mickey, Dave, and James scramble up into the wagon retrieving their gear. Mickey very quickly has his things off the wagon and his precious enlistment paper in his hand. James is next, and he and Mickey are frozen at attention looking straight ahead. David has his gear off the wagon but can't seem to find his papers. He's down on one knee tearing at his bag and clothing in desperation. Occasionally he looks up at Grounds as if to get some understanding.

Grounds walks over by where David is frantically searching for his papers, and with one movement, Grounds puts his big dirty boot against David's shoulder and pushes him over into the dirt. Grounds looks at Mickey.

"Ya know what you little shit? This is your lucky day. I was gonna take you for my little angel to make my bed and get my food and whatever else I may need. But your friend here has beat you out for the honor. He ain't as cute or young as you, but he'll do. Ya hear that?"

Grounds bends down nearly touching David's face with his.

"Ya hear that, Muffin? Keep on lookin for yer paper. You already won the honors to be my cherub if I need ya."

David barely looks up, and finally his search pays off with the papers. He springs to attention. Grounds passes in front of each one holding out his hand and collecting the enlistment papers. He looks through them and turns again toward Mickey.

"Listen, Pup. You ain't no eighteen year old, but if the Colonel says you are, then you are. And I'm gonna train the three of ya until you're assigned to yer first combat unit. But I ain't goin into no fight with some snot-nosed kid at my back or side. Hell, grown men piss themselves in fights. I just ain't ever gonna fight with the likes of ya and I pity the poor bastard that has to. Havin to fight along any of you three is a death sentence. Now, all I just said is true…that is until I train ya. You pass my trainin, or you'll be beggin to be dead. And I ain't shittin ya."

Mickey immediately figures he'll just stay low profile and learn everything he can. But he knows he must pass the training and eventually prove himself to Grounds even before he's in a real battle. But Mickey's focus is to prove his worth and be ready to fight alongside or protect Joe's back.

Grounds tucks the papers into his pants pocket and glances at the supply tent, "Now, stand at attention and I'm going to march you over to the supply area where you'll get your gear. Stand one behind the other, shortest up front and when I say the words ready march you all start out left foot first and follow me. After we start ya look down and make sure everybody's left foot is hittin the ground at the same time. Ya might of figured out that yer right ones oughta be hittin at the same time, too. When I want you to stop, I'll tell you to halt, and you'll stop and stay at attention until I tell you to be at ease. No talking. No lookin around. Okay, forward march."

The three walk behind Corporal Grounds and they are very aware many people stop and find it amusing to see three new guys in camp. The lack of uniforms makes them stick out like a sore thumb. They enter the uniform tent and Grounds gives them a final word, "You keep your mouths shut and your ears open. If one of these experts in here asks you a question, you answer. But you don't question what they give you. You take it and be glad you got all this stuff. Now go through this line, and I'll be waitin for ya at the other end. Don't none of ya fuck up and embarrass me. "

Grounds walks out the side of the tent and heads toward the other end farthest away from them. Mickey is first through the line and the first supply clerk motions for him to step forward. The man is so close Mickey can feel his breath...and smell his breath of onions and tobacco smoke. He has the most ill-fitting uniform imaginable, and this is his job. Already Mickey's expectations of uniforms is quickly going down. The clerk's cap is pulled down to where it rests on his ears. His hair sticks out from underneath and looks like it may never have seen a comb or soapy water. Apparently, the clerk can't see well because he gets very close to Mickey to examine him for size. He looks Mickey up and down from head to toe. He momentarily disappears into stacks of uniforms and brings back an armload of clothing. It can't possibly fit, but Mickey takes it.

The young soldier behind the counter says to Mickey, "You just got all the clothes you're gonna need for the next year. Sure ya want to keep carryin that stuff ya brought from home except for what yer wearin? Anything ya don't want just give it to me now or later, and it will be given to home folks that may be in need. Mickey puts his small tote bag on the counter and indicates for the man to take it.

Then Mickey moves on down the line. Another supply clerk walks from behind the counter and using a smooth stick with numbers on it, measures Mickey's foot width and length. Then he disappears and brings back a pair of boots. The laces are tied together, and the man drapes the lace around Mickey's neck, so the boots are hanging in front and resting on the armload of clothes. The next man has Mickey walk over to a counter, the clothes are briefly counted and put into a huge burlap bag. A rope is tied at each end of the bag and hung on Mickey's shoulder. Much easier to carry everything but still quite a load and they don't even have guns yet.

At the next station, a man brings out another burlap bag already tied at each end, places it on Mickey's left shoulder and motions for him to exit the tent toward where Corporal Grounds awaits. Mickey walks up within a few paces of Corporal Grounds and stands at attention.

Grounds looks at Mickey for a second, "Take a load off, Kid. At ease. Drop those bags and boots until the others are done."

Mickey thinks for a second that Grounds had just been playing tough as sort of an act, but before he has time to consider the thought, Grounds walks out into the roadway where two soldiers are walking, and Grounds deliberately trips and pushes one of them to the gravel. Grounds reaches down and pulls the man up by his shirt collar and bellows at him, "Larson, you fuckin buttercup! Ya better dream tonight of how to fight man-to-man like I tried teachin you. Far as I'm concerned you ain't passed my trainin and you sure as hell ain't no soldier I'd want to go into a fight with. But President

Davis says he needs ya now, so you better get a backbone real quick. Otherwise, yer gonna be dead or yer gonna turn tail and run off as a deserter. Course if ya desert I'll hope to get the pleasure of bein on your firing squad. Get outta my sight."

Grounds spits and then walks back over by Mickey as if nothing has happened. Grounds doesn't seem to want to talk, and Mickey thinks it best just to be silent.

Fairly soon all three new soldiers are finished with the supply exercise and ready for Grounds next adventure for them. He has them pick up their belongings and instructs them to march behind him to their "new home" as Grounds calls it. They walk through a dizzying jumble of tents, lines of mumbling men, and more lines of tents. Soldiers look up and occasionally walk to the outside of the tent and either nod a greeting or chuckle at the new guys. At one point Grounds points to another long, open-sided tent nearby. A line snakes out of one end of the tent where the soldiers are each carrying a metal dish for their food.

"In the one bag, you got a mess kit. It's a plate, cup and spoon. Ya ain't getting a knife or fork cause ya might injure yourself and we don't like government property getting damaged. This is your tent right up here and if I was you, for which I'm glad I ain't, since you're such a sorry bunch of peckerheads, anyhow I'd dig out the mess kit in one of those bags ya got and then head on down to this tent to get something to eat. Yer still in time for chow. This ain't like home, and your momma ain't gonna fix ya something every time ya get hungry. We eat when bells ring. When the bell rings three times, you grab your kit and get yer ass in line to eat. When the bell rings two times it means if you ain't in line you better get there quick and then the bell rings once and Sergeant Cookie brings the last man in line a pan painted red to bring through the line, and he's the last one to eat. That's it till next meal."

Grounds stops at a tent with four metal beds. There are thin, lumpy mattresses rolled up on one end of each bed. The four walls of the tent are rolled up next to the roof and tied up.

Pick a bunk, get your mess kit, and get somethin to eat. The latrine is straight out past your tent a couple hundred yards. Yer lucky about that too. Ain't good to be too close. After ya eat, get yer bunks fixed and uniforms tried on. Today is to get ya ready with all the bullshit stuff. Tomorrow is trainin. Tonight the bugle call for days end is at ten. From now on, at that time, lanterns are out and you can either leave up the tent walls or put em down. Don't matter. But don't put the walls down and have those lanterns lit, cause the sentries will catch that and come get me to teach ya some discipline. And ya don't want to make Corporal Grounds get up late at night because I get really nasty when I get woke up to dispense discipline. So get somethin to eat. I'll be back later to see how yer doin."

Mickey and his two newfound associates do as Grounds suggests and dig out their mess kits, taking the metal plate that doubles as a bowl, a spoon and quickly head for the mess tent.

The Sergeant of the mess is easy to spot. He's sitting at a table to the side of the line watching every person who comes through. He is grossly fat and unshaven. Though he appears ready to pounce on some unsuspecting soul, he remains quiet and learing.

Mickey is expecting some food for breakfast like eggs or bacon. He's surprised by the quantity of white beans, turnip greens and cornbread loaded on his plate. Mickey shrugs his shoulders and carries his heaped plate back to his tent and David volunteers to watch over the plates if Mickey and James will run back and get them each some coffee. Mickey and James soon discover that boiling coffee is not easy to carry in a large tin cup and it's even more difficult to juggle two cups. They quickly note how most other soldiers carry a towel or underwear shirt to use as a potholder for hot plates and cups. Lesson learned day one.

They make up their bunks and Mickey heads for the toilet, which he now knows is what Grounds refers to as the latrine. Pretty easy to spot. A trench about two feet deep and a foot wide running a couple hundred feet long. The dirt from the trench is mounded up on one side of the trench and shovels are stuck in the dirt every ten feet or so. Mickey sees how the others use the trench and then toss a shovel of dirt to cover the results of the visit. Mickey finds it's amazing how the army figured out this latrine system as they call it. He had always wondered if soldiers just found a private spot in the woods or if there were a hundred outhouses in camps. Lesson two day one.

As the afternoon hours approach, they feel the day's exhausting result, so Mickey and his partially uniformed tent mates lay quietly on their beds and Mickey realizes he's made it through most of the first day as a soldier. He wonders how his ma is doing and he pictures each of his brothers and sisters as they are told that Mickey has joined up with Joe. Mickey has a smile on his face as he drifts off in a little nap.

A familiar voice is louder than a bugle and brings Mickey back to the reality that he's not at home but in the army.

"Get your sorry asses outta those beds!"

Mickey, David, and James lurch from the sound and land unsteadily on their feet trying to make sense of what's happening.

"You lazy assholes would still be snuggled in your cribs takin the afternoon off if'n I hadn't come by to play Mammy Hen. Now listen up! Get yer uniforms on and get your beds made ready for my inspection. You get that done, come outside here, stand in a line at ease until I come and see how things look. If everything passes muster for me, then I'll leave ya alone until tomorrow's trainin. Otherwise, we'll be doin some corrective instruction on maintainin yer area. Ya got thirty minutes and not a second longer so get at it, Ladies."

Mickey scrambles around straightening his uniform, and then, on go the socks and boots. To his astonishment, everything fits as well as any clothes he's ever owned. In fact, Mickey smiles because these are the first clothes he's ever had that weren't hand-me-downs from Joe or older neighbor boys. This is his. The uniform of Michael Sean O'Day.

Mickey straightens his bed covers and puts most of his issued articles in the bags and sets them beside his bed. Mickey heard once from Joe that bed covers are supposed to be stretched tight, so he tries his best, and eventually the three go outside their tent and stand in a line. There's no conversation because they are still rattled by Corporal Ground's intrusion. Mickey can see the lumbering hulk of Corporal Grounds coming their way.

"Tench Hut!" Grounds is right in front of them less than three feet away, but he chooses to yell as if they are deaf or a hundred yards away. Mickey can smell tobacco and a hint of what is likely rotgut whiskey. He used to smell it on his dad.

"You three turn around right where you are when I give you a command to about-face, and then you stay in line at attention. That way you can see my inspection and what I look for. Okay ABOOOUT... FACE!!!"

Awkwardly the three try to turn in place, turning different directions, off balance, and then quickly recovering facing Grounds. The big corporal surveys the inside of the tent and turns back toward the three.

In a normal tone, he says, "We're gonna get this about-face down before I go any farther. Ya put yer right toe behind yer left foot and turn like this. Go ahead just do it a couple of times."

Mickey gets it right away and resumes his stance at attention. Grounds stops the other two, gives the command again and now all three are doing a proper about-face.

"Awright. Now we'll see how army ready you three are. Ready for inspection?"

Mickey nods his head, and James makes the mistaken verbal response, "Yes, Sir."

Grounds takes a huge step and puts his forehead on Jame's forehead and screams, "I ain't no Sir. Never have been and never will be. I wasn't handed this rank under no table. I earned it, and I am Corporal to you. You stupid or trying to make me mad? Huh? Which is it?"

"I'm stupid, Si...Corporal."

Grounds turns away and walks directly to one of the beds. "Each of youse stand at attention at the foot of your bed."

The three comply quickly.

Grounds walks to Mickey's bed. He folds the corners of the blankets and tucks them in a bit tighter. He puts the pillow centered at the head of the bed and folds the top of the blanket back to the front edge of the pillow. Grounds grabs Mickey's two bags and takes them to the foot of the bed, shoves Mickey out of the way and puts the bags at the foot of the bed. He takes Mickey by the shoulders and moves him back in front of the bags and then turns to the other two.

"The pup done good and this man don't say that very often. This is the way your tent will look every morning you're with me. Got it."

In unison, "Yes, Corporal."

Grounds smiles. "Music to my ears, boys. Music to my ears. You just might be trainable. Now in a little while,

I'm goin to the chow tent with whoever's got their bed fixed just like the kid. Now let's start fresh."

Grounds walks over to both of the other two beds, pushes the two soldiers out of his way, flips the beds upside down and dumps the entire contents out of their bags on the bottom side of the bed.

"Get at it. Ten minutes. Pup can help ya'll if he has a mind to. Up to you, Pup, but in 10 minutes I'm comin back to see how these other two are doin."

Mickey can hardly believe his ears. Grounds is actually showing him a little respect, or at the very least he did okay. Mickey doesn't trust the corporal, but it certainly could be worse. He pitches in and helps David and James finish their beds the way they should be. The three go outside the tent and wait for Grounds. In anticipation of a favorable reaction, they all three carry their plate, cup, a spoon, and an undershirt to hold the hot containers once they are filled.

Grounds comes lumbering toward them carrying a tin cup of coffee. He stops, looks into the tent, takes a swig of coffee, wipes his beard and turns toward the three waiting soldiers.

"Let's go get some grub. No marchin, just walk behind me and no talkin. Eat your food, secure your mess kit and wait in your tent. In an hour we're goin to march over and get the tools of our trade for you."

Mickey, James and David follow Grounds instructions and soon they've finished eating, stored their mess kits and are marching, mostly in step with Grounds, over to the armory. It is one of the few actual buildings not a tent but a rather miserable sight. Probably somebody's old abandoned farm shed at one time and now painted with so many coats of whitewash it looks as though the surface is made of marshmallows. As they enter the building, they take their places in a short line passing by a counter very similar to when they were issued uniforms and gear.

Mickey is surprised. He's handed an old double barrel shotgun, and as he glances behind him, he sees that David and James are given the same. Mickey wonders if these are just for some sort of training and they'll get long rifles later. Next, they are each handed a spike-like bayonet, and Mickey hesitates as he looks at it quickly drawing the attention of the clerk behind the counter.

"What's your problem? Not to your likin? Maybe you thought you'd get an officer's sword?"

Grounds quickly steps in, "Pick up that bayonet, kid. I don't want to hear a word. Wait outside at attention."

Marching back to the tent Mickey begins to feel stomach cramps. He has a cold sweat and is struggling to keep from doubling over from the surging pains. As the little group reaches the tent Grounds instructs, "Okay, boys, secure your equipment by your bunks and ya can play with any of the stuff here inside yer tent but not outside. I don't want ya hurtin somebody." Grounds actually laughs at his own joke.

Mickey can hardly stand the onset of what he knows is going to be diarrhea as the big Corporal edges his way toward the front of the tent. Grounds turns one last time, "I may not see ya boys anymore this fine evening so you rest up as good as ya can cause we're gonna start real training at the crack of dawn. You get up with reveille, uniform for tomorrow is boots, pants, undershirt, and cap, straighten those bunks for inspection and then grab some grub. I'll be looking for you three ready for inspection and ready for trainin an hour after reveille. Got it?"

"Yes, Corporal," comes in unison.

"Ah, music to my ears, boys. Music to my ears."

As soon as the corporal clears the front flap of the tent, all three began to squirm and groan with obvious lower digestive discomfort and Mickey is first out of the tent running for the latrine. He runs right past Grounds, and he's sure he hears Grounds laugh a bit but Mickey feels so sick he can't care at this point. There is a crowd running toward and arriving around the latrine. He makes it to the ditch just in time, unbuttoned upon arrival.. It's a line of exposed bottoms, inglorious sounds, and groans. Personal embarrassment isn't a consideration and looking around has absolutely no appeal The intestinal pains hit Mickey in waves , and it feels like relief isn't going to be lightning fast. Once, then a second time Mickey feels a bit better. He gingerly buttons up his pants, takes his place in the line by the hand pump to wash his hands, only to feel a painful surge and be right back over the trench of stench. .Repeated attempts to hurry the process and button up only get him a couple of steps until he must quickly find another spot in the line of bare bottoms.

Eventually, Mickey seems to be feeling like his bout of dysentery is about over, and he feels so weak he can barely stand and slowly walk toward his tent. What a way to start combat training. Mickey feels weak, tremendously thirsty and really squeamish. As Mickey walks slowly into his tent, Grounds is lying on James's bed with a big grin on his face.

"You momma's boys is all alike. Happens with every new group of volunteers. Your second meal ate out of a mess kit that was likely dipped in that soapy water outside the mess tent but never really warshed proper-like and certainly, that old lye soap never renched-off proper either. Bad warshin and bad renchin. And now ya'll got the green apple quickstep or like I say ya'all got the shits, ain't ya? How ya like that?"

"I 'm sorry Corporal. I never thought..."

"Take it easy, kid. You all catch a break tonight. Happens with some in every new group and it's not likely something you'll forget. Wait for your two buddies. I'm sure they was raised with a sugar tit and never thought about how their old Mammys was a warshin and a-renchin dishes for good reason and not just to keep their fingernails clean. I'm sure your buddies will have turned themselves inside out pretty quick and then they'll come back to see what the big bad Corporal's gonna do to em."

"What about the training tomorrow, Corporal Grounds?"

"Just hold your question. I think I hear a little whimperin and groanin comin toward the tent."

Sure enough, the tent flap pulls back and in the outside light are the silhouettes of David and James, holding across their bellies like they'd been shot. Grounds stands and towers over the three.

"Alright, Boys. Sit on your bunks and listen to me. From now on, the first thing you do after you eat is go back by the mess tent and use the soapy water and warsh them metal plates and spoons off real good. I seen all y'all dip your plates in that soap but I never saw a one of ya scrub them plates with your hands, and I never saw a one of ya rench that soap off good and proper at the hand pump. If you leave food or soap on your eatin tools, you'll get the shits. You get into Yankee territory, and you'd either be unable to defend yourself, or you'd get sniped dead while you're astraddle of that ditch. This is an important lesson. Now, youse rest, drink water and when you feel a little better go wash them mess kits like I told ya. If ya feel like it, eat a little breakfast in the mornin but don't force it or eat too much. Our mornin plans are still your orders. Rest up. Drink water. We got plenty to do in the mornin. Got it?"

In unison, "Yes, Corporal Grounds."

Grounds starts out of the tent and then turns. "Don't you three ever...and I mean ever let this happen again. You'll likely be dead and so might some of your brothers in battle. Them God- damned Yanks like nothin better than to slaughter rebs who can't hardly stand up on their own pegs. So get well, and get ready to learn."

The three quietly groan as they lay back on their bunks and not a word is spoken.

Recovery is slow for the next couple hours but as the ten o'clock hour approaches all are a little weak but otherwise feeling back to normal.

Only a couple of days of being soldiers and already the routine is met like thousands of soldiers before them. Reveille sounds and from Mickey's tent are a few quiet curses, a few groans, and sounds of beds being made. Mickey and his tent-mates get some breakfast, carefully wash their mess kits and ready themselves for the day ahead.

Soon Grounds reappears with two canvas bags, straps slung over his shoulder. "Okay follow me to our trainin spot so we can get started."

They walk without trying to march, juggling and jangling the shotguns and loose bayonets trying to figure if there is a proper or convenient way to carry both. Mickey carries the shotgun in his right hand with the stock under his armpit. That's the way he did at home when he was squirrel or rabbit hunting. He walks and examines the bayonet.

Corporal Grounds slows his pace and holds up his hand for his soldiers to stop. He walks back to them and shakes his head, "You guys don't even try to be soldiers do ya? Shoulder those guns on yer right shoulder and carry the other stuff in yer left hand. Okay, now let's move out again."

There's no way Mickey can see how the bayonet in his left hand is supposed to attach to a shotgun. Being puzzled probably makes the walk seem quicker than it would otherwise have been. The four leave the edge of the camp on a well-worn path about ten feet wide and soon come to a clearing. There are several straw bales around the clearing, and with a surprising action, Grounds dumps both canvas bags he's been carrying.

"Come here close where you can see."

From the contents of one bag Grounds picks up a strange looking metal object. He takes David's shotgun, breaks the breach, and then turns the barrel toward himself. He slips the metal object over the end of the barrels, slides it toward the stock and tightens a thumbscrew, loosens it and demonstrates how it will slide up and down the barrel and can be tightened at any point. He takes David's bayonet and snaps it onto the device, slides it down the barrel, so the tip of the bayonet sticks no more than about an inch beyond the end of the shotgun barrel. Then he takes off the bayonet, removes the clamp and tosses the clamp on the ground with the others. He hands David's shotgun back to him.

"Here's what were learnin here. Learn it good. I breached this shotgun to be sure it's empty. You don't ever take a gun from somebody or turn your own gun with the business end towards ya without makin sure it's safe. There's plenty of Yanks trying to kill ya without takin a load from one of yer own or yerself. Got that? Any questions?"

All three nod they understand.

"These are your guns from now on until you're either issued another weapon at your assigned regiment, or you take one off a blue-belly on the field. I might add, if you take a Yank's gun, he's gonna get a spankin from his Sergeant back in camp for losin his weapon so do him a favor and make sure he's dead when ya try to take it. Some Yanks play possum so be careful around battlefields. Now listen to this. If you don't know if a yank is dead, take your bayonet and gently touch one of his closed eyes. If he's alive he can't keep from his eyes flitchin. If he's alive, stick him until no eyes a twitching. Any questions?"

James speaks up before thinking, "So Corporal Grounds, this is my gun? We don't turn em in when we leave training?"

"That's right, sweetheart. That's your gun, and you'd best pay attention to me of how to fight with it. Next, you take a bayonet clamp and slip it over the barrels like I did, with this clip pointing forward." Each of the others begin to fasten the clamp to their shotgun. "Obviously these clamps I brought out here are made for the doubles, and there are others made for single barrel shotguns. You're lucky. You got double barrels, and that's one more shot than most."

Without much delay, all have the clamps in place.

"Be sure ya don't tighten that thumb screw too tight...but not too loose either. We'll get to that in two shakes of a sheep's tail. Now snap them bayonets onto the clamps."

Grounds watches as each man snaps his bayonet in place.

"The bayonet point cannot stick more than an inch beyond the end of the barrel, or you're gonna shoot your own bayonet. Adjust them like I said...okay that's fine. Now here's how all this works. Shotgun platoons see close combat. Artillery first. Rifles move forward firing volleys, and shotgun platoons are right behind the rifles. When the command is given for you guys, you charge past the riflemen, and you have two shots to spray blue-boys. If you can reload and fire again, you do so. But don't be fumbling around lookin for shells and have some Yank stick a sword or bayonet in yer craw. Boys this is what fightin's all about. If ya ain't got time to reload, ya slide that bayonet forward, and now ya tighten that lever on the clamp so tight ya grunt. Now ya begin the almighty fightin fer real. At this point, ya keep stickin and stickin. Listen to the bugle calls so ya know whether to keep plowin ahead, stop or get outta the way of our cavalry who'll cut em down as they try to run away. Any questions?"

David's hands are shaking, and he seems a little puzzled when he speaks, "So we're gonna learn those bugle calls, and I guess there's one for retreat, too?"

With one movement, Corporal Grounds hits David in the jaw and knocks him to the ground. Grounds bends over and lifts him by his shirt collar until his face is only inches from the corporal's, "Retreat is not a word you ever use in my presence! We charge! We fight forward! We stop when we've won! We move outta the way for a cavalry charge! That's it! And there better not be any more questions with that word. Do not ever use that word around me. You understand?"

"Yes, Corporal."

"Awright. Put those guns on your right shoulder and stand at attention. Hand me your gun, Irish."

Mickey quickly takes the gun from his shoulder, breaks the breach and hands the gun to Corporal Grounds. Grounds responds with a big ear-to-ear smile.

"Irish, you somethin alright. You may be a little guy, but you pay attention, and I hope you man enough to be a good soldier for these Confederate States."

Grounds closes the gun and moves the bayonet to its extended position. He stands in front of the three facing to the side. He lunges forward with the bayonet about chest high, makes a twisting circle with the point and then pulls back the gun holding it waist high. Grounds looks at his three charges and slowly repeats the demonstration. He accentuates the twisting circle after the lunge.

"Okay, see what I do after I stab with the bayonet. I twist, and as best I can do a little circle with the tip of the shiv. When you stab somebody with a bayonet a couple of things will happen. The Yank you stab will react by grabbing the gun and bayonet. Just a defensive reaction because I'm told it hurts a good bit to get stuck in the gut. Also, there may be times when you stab somebody through a bone or joint, and the bayonet gets stuck for a second. You don't have time to screw around with it in either case. You thrust like lightning, you twist as hard as ya can, and you pull back like lightning. And you sure as hell don't want some screamin Yank stuck on the other end. You gotta be ready for the next one before they get you. Now, we're gonna practice this til you got the idea. Spread apart, so's ya don't stab each other and show me what ya learned."

Mickey is still glowing from Grounds' compliment, so he does as instructed without paying much attention to the other two. Mickey is going through the motions and Grounds comes over beside him.

"Listen, son. You've got the right moves on this but show me ya can kill. Picture some ugly Yank havin his way with your Ma, and you get him stood up in front of ya. Show me, Irish!"

Mickey lunges with a horrific scream, makes the right twist technique with his bayonet and then stabs again and again before he stops, somewhat embarrassed that he got carried away.

"That's my boy, Irish. Okay, I wanna see you, Mitchell. Go ahead."

David lunges as if a little unsure, pauses, twists the tip and withdraws to the ready position.

"C'mon. Show me some fight. Do it again. D'you hear what I told O'Day? Do it. Picture somebody and kill em. Now, ***do it***!'

David does the demonstration with more intensity, and Grounds smiles at him. Grounds then turns to James and tells him to show what he's learned. James yells when he lunges and then returns to the ready position without twisting the bayonet.

Grounds puts his hand on James's shoulder and smiles, " Now I want you to charge that bale of straw at your full speed and stab that bale as if it's a Yank and then like lightnin move over and stab the next bale there just to the right of that one and then the third one. Now go!"

James charges the straw bale yelling at the top of his lungs, he rams the bayonet all the way in and recovers. He charges at the second bale screaming with some confidence. He rams the bayonet all the way in but when he tries to pull it back it is stuck, and when he pulls a second time his hands slip completely from the gun and as if to recover his mistake he grabs the gun again, still failing to twist the bayonet and this time he pulls the bale over onto himself, and he stumbles backward and falls.

Grounds is uncharacteristically calm.

"Yeah, Boys, this is practice. This is training. But you have to listen and do these things right. There are wooden planks baled inside some of this straw, so if you don't twist hard and pull that bayonet back, you see what happens. You won't get a second chance in real combat, so we're gonna practice this a few more times. Mitchell, you go next and do it right. Okay?"

Finally, all three soldiers satisfactorily demonstrate that the Corporal's point is taken.

"Okay boys, here's six shotgun shells for each of ya. Put four in your pocket and load those shotguns. Anybody who don't know how to shoot a double barrel? So don't let me see none of ya's blastin both barrels at the same time." Grounds looks at each, and they seem to be familiar with shotguns. "So here's what I want ya to do. See that post over to the left of the straw bales. We're gonna back up, and then I want ya one at a time to run toward that post and when you get to where we are right here you shoot the shit outta that post...one barrel at a time, please. After you fire the second shot, run that bayonet out and stab all three bales. Twist those bayonets. C'mon boys, show me ya got some fight in ya. Boyle, you go first. Let's walk back to the starting point and when I tell you, load them guns up but don't cock them until it's your turn and then you cock it while you're running toward the post. Let's go, boys."

They walk back to the starting point, and Grounds gives the order to load and lock the breach.

They each take turns learning to shoot and lunge with the bayonet, and each man improves with the speed and efficiency of sliding the bayonet at the proper time and locking it in place. Mickey again shows he's the star because from his experience of hunting he is able with shotgun accuracy to get the shots off while holding the gun at his side and never having to shoulder it to fire. He also doesn't stop running to shoot. Mickey simply slows to a smooth jog and fires both shots always hitting the post to the maximum. Grounds brings out more shells, and they continue to practice until the corporal calls a halt to the day's training.

"Boys, you are improving. Yes, indeed. All three of ya are doing just fine and Irish, we need to quit now and give that post some recovery time. It's got enough of your lead in it to weigh a ton. Good shootin, Irish."

Grounds looks at the three standing like baby birds waiting to be fed some more. He smiles a little, "Okay, Boys, that's enough for today. Y'all go on back to yer quarters. Take a load off til chow. Unless there's something I don't know, I'll just plan on seein ya when the bugle blows in the mornin."

As the three walk back toward the camp there's an air of satisfaction. David chuckles, "Shit, boys, I feel like I'm relaxin a bit around Grounds. My jaw still hurts like hell where he whopped me, but I feel like I sort of got the idea as we practiced. I actually feel more like a soldier."

Mickey responds, "Well, you sure look like a soldier, a good soldier."

The following morning Mickey, Dave, and James are laughing and talking with an air of confidence as if they have earned their way into the brotherhood of arms with exactly one evening of catastrophic dysentery and one day of Corporal Ground's training under their belts. After breakfast and successful inspection of their bunks, the three follow Corporal Grounds toward a different training area. Today they are to learn hand-to-hand fighting.

Corporal Grounds talks through what he calls some skills of fighting and Mickey listens but is thinking how his brother Joe's fighting techniques seem a whole lot more skillful. Grounds tires of his own demonstration rather quickly and rubs his hands together in triumph over his imaginary enemy.

"Got that you mutts?"

"Yes, Corporal Grounds," is the echo in three-part harmony.

“Watch it again. Get this straight in yer mind,” As Grounds demonstrates in slow motion with David how to block a punch and then throw a big haymaker.

Grounds pauses and gives an ear to ear grin showing his filthy yellow teeth. The best-looking part of his smile is the teeth that are missing. He growls,” This is when old Groundsie gets a little fun. Each of ya is gonna fight me man-to-man using what I just showed ya...twice. This is practice, but if I can knock ya out with my fists, I’m gonna. Okay? Who’s first?”

Slowly Mickey raises his hand, “Guess I can, Corporal.”

“Irish ya got guts. I’ll say that, but I’m tellin ya right now I ain’t holdin back on none of ya’s. So step up here, and we’re gonna fight...just like on the field. Ya sure as hell can’t run around a battlefield tryin to find somebody yer own size. When there’s no weapons, no knives, it’s jest you and him. C’mon, Irish, what ya got?”

Mickey knows exactly what he’s heard from Joe, “Protect your face and liver or at least the ribs on yer lower right side. When you’re pretty sure you’re gonna get hit, move toward the punch rather than away from it. If you’re fortunate the opponent’s blow will glance and now you’re close enough the other guy’s lost any size advantage. Then you hit hard and fast. That advantage doesn’t last but a second.”

Mickey puts his hands up, and so does Grounds. Grounds is obviously looking for one big hit to lay Mickey out. Mickey takes a deep breath and instead of circling or hesitating he strikes like lightning. Mickey screams so loud it’s shocking to Grounds and the two onlookers. Mickey charges forward before Grounds is ready and steps down as hard as he can on Ground's right foot. Mickey hits Grounds just like he did Elmer Hoenisch and at the same time pushes Grounds backward. Grounds hands fly out to the side as he loses his balance and then clumsily falls on his back on the ground. Mickey moves forward and stands over Grounds. He lets out another blood-curdling scream and then puts his fists down.

Grounds rolls over onto his hands and knees. He shakes his head a little and wipes his mouth and nose with his sleeve. He slowly gets to his feet and turns to face the others.

Grounds smiles a full smile through a bloody nose and mouth, "Men, Groundsie can take as well as give, and I just had my shit handed back to me. Irish, don't know where ya learned to fight and I don't care. You are now the third person out of all the hundreds I've trained here ever to lay me out. Good job, young man. I'm proud of ya. That scream threw me fer a loop right off, and you hit mighty hard for a whelp. Good job." Grounds pauses and looks at Jim and David, "Now who wants to try and be the fourth one to knock old Groundsie down?"

Jim and David try to pull off what they've learned that day, but it doesn't work out well. David gets flattened but gets up, and hoping to capture a bit of Mickey's skill, rushes Grounds screaming but instead of a glancing blow, David gets a fist right under the chin, and his feet actually leave the ground as he is knocked out. Jim fairs little better.

Grounds calls a stop to the training as a lone horseman slowly makes his way across the field toward them. Grounds rubs his nose, "Looks like we got company so we'll take a break. Y'all tried to show what I demonstrated, but it's tough to make it all work the first time. Now ya don't need to be pickin no fights just to practice, but I want ya to think about today and be ready to do it right when the time comes. Irish, ya little shit, I'll take my lesson from you today or at least until my sore beak gets better. Now just who in hell's bells is this a comin?"

Grounds recognizes the man on horseback, "Top Sergeant Turnbull. Come out to check trainin?"

"Groundsie, I hope yer trainin is as good as you always claim. Is this Mitchell, Boyd and O'Day?"

"That they are, Top." Grounds turns to the three, "Boys, this here's one of the CSA's finest. This is Regimental Sergeant Major Owen Turnbull. The Top Sergeant in this regiment."

"Okay, Groundsie, enough of the introductions. Your three trainees have orders to move out tomorrow to an active combat Tennessee Regiment. They'll finish training there. One hour after reveille you be in uniform outside your quarters with your assigned gun, and all yer stuff packed ready to go."

There's dead silence from the surprise and just as nonchalantly as his approach a few moments ago, Sergeant Major Turnbull turns and walks his horse at the same slow gait toward another training area. Grounds repeats Sergeant Turnbull's instructions to his charges.

That evening after chow, Grounds appears at Mickey's tent. Corporal Grounds resembling a big sentimental bully has his final words before lights out and says, "Boys, you've done well, and I hope ya learnt somethin from me. Last year guys like you were here practicin combat for a month. Y'all got a couple of days, and we can only hope that helps. Stay alive and keep the guys next to ya alive. Look sharp. Make me proud."

The next morning it's exactly like Grounds said, they are waiting by their tent, and a Regimental Corporal comes by, reads their names and off they go. When they march up to the circular drive in front of the headquarters building, their wagon awaits and they load their gear and climb in along with nine others. Twelve in all are moving out for Fort Davis, just north of the Mississippi State line and South of Memphis.

There are two soldiers to drive the wagon, and one of them turns and addresses the troops in the back of the wagon. "Boys, my name's Polk...Private Edward Polk. And this other'n is Private George Berry. Just remember Polk Berry. Ya know them red berries that birds shit all over yer old lady's white sheets hangin on the line. Only reason ya need to know our names is if ya get sick or gotta dump. And if we stop for either of those, make it quick. Otherwise, we keep a movin. Me and Berry take turns drivin. Meals will happen when Polk and Berry gets hungry and it ain't much food-wise but damn sight better'n nothin. Good chow will be when we get to camp. Now, while we're movin ya can sleep, ya can talk but no drinkin, gamblin or fightin. If ya gotta pee just go out the back of the wagon. But two things about that. First, check the wind direction cause yer liable to make somebody real mad if ya get it wrong.

Second, if ya fall outta the wagon while standing back there, run like hell and catch up. We have to deliver all twelve of ya, but we try to keep a pace that will get us where we are a goin in thirty hours. Y'all are soldiers, so load yer guns. Don't expect no trouble but from time to time we run into a Yank patrol or a little gang of deserters. In either case, we need to kill them afore they get a chance to kill us. So if ya see something strange holler out."

The trip is uneventful, boring and painful. It's late afternoon of the second day as the wagon pulls up to the guard shack at the new camp boundary. The guard takes the orders and other papers from Berry. Mickey was sleeping, but he raises up and looks over the wagon sideboard. The guard with the papers is within just a few feet, and Mickey can tell the guard is holding the papers upside down. The guard likely can't read, but he officiously looks over them and hands them back to Berry, "Here ya go, Georgie-Boy. All looks in order."

Berry smiles and gives a half-hearted salute to the guard.

Arrival at Fort Davis feels like a repeat of Camp Whitespring except Mickey and the other new assignees don't stand out like new recruits. They are quickly assigned three to a tent and so Mickey, David and James once again bunk together. Like old times.

David yells to a passing soldier, "Hey Buddy, any chance of gettin chow at this hour or are we too late?"

"Never too late for Sergeant Cookie. Long as he's got a little shine in his coffee mug, he'll whip ya up somethin day or night. Good guy. Says he's only afraid of makin us so fat we can't fight, and then he'll have ta fight.

Outta yer tent make a left and go about fifty yards. Can't miss it."

"Hey, thanks."

"Don't mention it. Now ya owe me. So maybe ya can save my life someday."

As Mickey and his comrades are settling into their new surroundings, a man enters their tent, "Good day to ya, soldiers. I'm First Sergeant Denman, and you're assigned to my company, Bravo Company...B Company. In the morning at reveille get your bunks in shape, uniforms on, get some chow and when assembly sounds report to the assembly grounds. No weapons tomorrow. Clean em tonight and leave em on yer bunk. You won't have trouble findin the assembly grounds cause it's where everybody's goin tomorrow. Our company is easiest to find. As you face the flag on the assembly area, we are front two rows all the way on the left side. When you get there, fall in, and Corporal Hadley will be takin roll. Got it?"

In unison, "Yes Sergeant."

So beds are made, gear sorted, guns unloaded, a plateful of real food from "Cookie" and the night draws to a close.

Long before the sun even hints a peek over the Eastern horizon, the lone, distant bugle call sounds. It's the first notice that within minutes buglers all over the camp will be mustered to be sure the troops are pried from the night's sleep. The first call is enough to evoke a unisoned groan throughout the camp because it's the first hint that reveille will be played at exactly five in the morning, about fifteen minutes from now. Mickey sits up on his cot, stretches, and yawns. James and David follow suit. Within a few minutes, they are dressed and outside their tent headed for the mess tent.

Later in the morning another bugle call starts faintly at the brigade General's area, soon echoed by the regimental bugler and then the company buglers. Mickey, David, and James are not familiar with the calls but soon find out the last one is a call to report to the assembly area for the day's work details.

As the men assemble at least part of the mystery of the day's activities is solved. There are shovels piled in front of each company's assembly point. After Corporal Hadley takes roll, the men are quickly formed into work parties and ordered to "right-shoulder arms" command with a shovel. Mickey is shocked at how many men are marching in a long line toward the edge of the camp. They continue to march on a two-rutted dirt road through a woods and onto a clearing about three miles from camp. At the very edge of the woods, they are ordered to build a dirt revetment similar to a levee often found along a river to prevent flooding. But this is being built between the edge of a woods and a long open field.

By the day's end, the task is completed thanks to the mobile mess that brings them dinner right to the work area. As they march back to camp with shovels over their shoulders, Mickey is so exhausted he would give anything to lie down on his cot and take a nap, a long nap. But after the return to camp, a cold soak in the nearby creek feels more refreshing. Word around camp is that the general is very pleased with the revetment and it is finished for the moment.

After reveille and breakfast the next day Mickey groans aloud as he hears the bugle call for assembly. It's easy to see the piles of shovels are ready again today and the procedure seems to be the same. This time as they reach the clearing, they are sent over the revetment and ordered to fill bags of dirt and stack them about two-feet thick against the front of the revetment. Word spreads quickly that there is an expected battle in defense of the camp and it is will likely occur within just a few days.

They return to camp once again and are wondering what they could possibly dig tomorrow. The next day, much to Mickey and everyone else's surprise they meet at the assembly point, take roll and spend the morning hours marching and drilling battlefield commands. The bugle calls for battles and skirmishes are explained and played again and again. The final instruction before noon is for each man to come fully armed for the afternoon work and drill time.

The assembly area is quite a sight when everyone falls-in to their respective companies. Sergeant Denman and Corporal Hadley stand in front of Mickey's company and look slightly nervous.

Corporal Hadley steps forward, glances at his Sergeant and addresses Mickey's Company, "Tenn-Chut!! Fall in Boys. Get to attention and listen up. You better already know but just in case I'm Corporal Chris Hadley, and this is First Sergeant Luther Denman. We are your leaders for this Company. You are soldiers in Company

B as in Boys, Buggars, Balls, and Battle. Sergeant Denman, they're all yours."

Sergeant Denman and Corporal Hadley walk by the lined-up troops and pause in front of each one and check each name off their list. After assuring himself that everyone is present Sergeant Denman speaks in a calming voice, "Stand at ease, Boys. Now gather around us so you can see and hear. If we were at full strength, we'd have ninety of youse but as you can see we're a little short-handed. There are forty-two of ya."

The Sergeant takes a walking stick he had nearby and draws a straight line in the dirt.

"Men, this line is that back-breaking revetment you made in the last couple of days." He draws a big box a little ways away from the line. "This is where we are in camp. Okay?"

In unison, there was a quiet, "Yes, Sergeant."

"Alright then, over here this line is the Yanks coming this way wantin to run over us and take this camp and set up housekeepin in this entire area. But this battle we're preparing for is going to stop them dead in their tracks. And the word dead is what I mean. General Banks says we'll stop em, scatter em and run em down when they turn tail and run away. Our entire artillery battery will be behind this wonderful revetment you boys built. Infantry companies will be amassed to each side of our artillery line and concealed on both the right and left flanks in the woods. Cavalry will be right straight behind the artillery. The yanks will see the smoke from our big guns, and they'll be tryin to knock out our artillery. One by one our artillery will stop firin so's the Yanks think they've knocked em out. What they don't know is, we'll be re-sightin those big silent guns level with the battlefield just lyin in wait. The Yanks may pause for a bit, and then we expect they'll begin to march straight toward the line of guns. When they're drawn up close enough, our artillery will have re-sighted canons level with their infantry troops. When we've blown holes into their infantry line, our canons will re-sight once again to strike their rear lines and artillery again, and that's when you'll get the signal to charge. You brave infantrymen will attack from both flanks. That's from the sides for you new guys. Then while we're attacking from the flanks, our cavalry will come straight over the revetment and engage the center of them and shoot them and stick them like the pigs they are. You understand?"

"Yes, Sergeant."

Mickey's heart is about to jump out of his shirt. He wanted to be like Joe and fight. Looks like it's coming up fast and he feels like he sure would like to have had about another week of combat training with Corporal Grounds.

David speaks up, "Sergeant, when will all this take place?"

"I'm getting to that, soldier, and the answer is from now on we are ordered to be ready. Whether it's day or night when the bugles sound assembly, you assemble here and bring your weapons for combat. You form up like mornings, you'll get more ammo so be sure you got your pouches with ya. I heard we may even assemble tomorrow at the regular morning time, march over there and wait for the Yanks. If we do, meals will come out by chuck wagon. The Yanks are close enough right now... at most two days away, and we don't know if they'll march all night to get into position thinking we won't be prepared. I know our artillery has been ordered to get into position tonight and we have advanced guards posted across that clearing to watch for the first sign of the Yanks. Boys, this'll be a good one for the Confederate States of America."

Mickey hears James and David tossing and turning during the night, and there's little sleep Mickey is able to catch. He's thinking, reviewing what Corporal Grounds told them. He tries to imagine what Joe would be telling him about now. Oh, if Mickey could go into this at Joe's side. This battle may present a chance to show his bravery. Mickey is too naïve to consider the negative results of battle.

As morning breaks, the events of the day take place exactly as Sergeant Denman suspected. They meet at the assembly area, get a supply of ammunition and march through the woods to the revetment area. As they approach their goal It's clear the artillery is already in place, and each cannon's crew is at the ready. Company Sergeants place their troops about a hundred yards from the last artillery piece on both the right and left flanks. Mickey is fascinated by how the cannons are set up. Work crews cut slots in the revetment so each cannon can fire at unlimited elevations, even ground level. The sandbags are packed so close on the sides it would take a direct hit on a cannon barrel to knock out an artillery piece. So now it's a waiting game. Mickey wonders if it will be as soon as tomorrow or the next day. This waiting is the worst part.

Mickey's jitters don't have to last long. A horseman can be seen at full gallop off to the left of the Confederate forces and coming for their line. He must be one of the advanced sentries with news of the Yanks. Behind the infantry lines, Mickey can hear a couple of horses trotting, stopping, orders being given and then moving on down the line. Sergeant Denman and Corporal Hadley stand in front of Mickey's company.

"Boys, the Yanks marched last night, and they're close. Our artillery is zeroed in on the distance out there to our front. You can't see too good from behind the revetment or over here, but there's a clump of trees and a little hill you can see a way out there in the distance. General Banks figures the Yanks will set their artillery in a line on either side of those farthest trees at first. That's about the range limit, and it may even be too far for them to hit us. The Yanks will come over that little hill, and they'll know pretty quick they need to set their artillery closer. They'll try to fortify it, and we think as they look over here all they'll see is this revetment. Before they get set up, our artillery will smash them. When our big guns are firin, Y'all just stay low and ready. I told ya how when the Yanks fire at us, our guns will go silent one by one to fake like they have hit our guns. They'll start movin their guns, and that's when the Yanks infantry and cavalry will form a battle line and charge us in the open. That's when our artillery will do a second volley of the big guns at man level and cut them som-bitches down. Then and only then will we get the signal to go. Their troops will be comin in a line across that entire field. It'll be loud and smoky, but you listen for the bugler. When you hear our bugler sound "charge", don't look around for me to tell you to go.

You go! And I'll be right with ya. God, how I love this!"

Word is passed to the troops that the food wagon is back in the woods a couple hundred yards and each company in turn breaks and goes quickly to the wagon, gets some meat, bread, and water and then returns to their assigned position to eat. Mickey's about to take his second bite of a sandwich he carefully prepared when he nearly jumps out of his skin from the loudest explosion he's ever heard. It's followed by the deafening sound of all the artillery shooting. Black smoke and the smell of gun powder is intense. This is how it begins.

Mickey drops his sandwich when a Yankee cannon shell rips through the trees behind them. The sound is ten times louder than any thunder he's ever heard.

"They're shootin too high! Heads down! Didn't think their fire would reach us but that's sure as hell, not the case. They'll lower it to the big guns in a minute...just stay down!"

Mickey mouths the words, "Yes Sergeant." But he can't tell if he made a sound or not because of the earsplitting explosions in front and behind.

It isn't long until the Union shells are hitting the revetment and dirt is showering from the sandbags. So far it looks like none of the rebel cannons are hit. There's the sound of a bugle, but it's a bugle call that's completely new. The soldiers begin to look around at Sergeant Denman to see what's happening. Sergeant Denman laughs nervously and yells to the men, "Hold yer ground. That ain't the call to charge. That call's only for the artillery. The old man's foolin the Blue-

Boys so when our canons, one-by-one stop firing and resight at man-level. We're getting close boys but hold yer ground! Watch and listen for the "Charge."

Sure enough in about twenty minutes, there's only a couple of the rebel artillery firing, but the silent canons are all standing by ready to fire when the union charge comes. It's apparent when the Union troops are lured into charging across the open field because all the "silent" artillery open up once again.

Sergeant Denman stands in front of the company. "Boys, stand up! Weapons ready! Any second now. Watch me and listen! Get ready to stick them blue pigs!"

The bugle call to charge is loud and Sergeant Denman and Corporal Hadley are waving their arms to charge. Mickey scurries a couple steps behind his sergeant. His first sight of the battlefield is blue uniforms about three hundred yards away, and some are lying on the ground. A few are charging ahead toward the cannons expecting the rebels to come over the revetments but many yanks are already in retreat and are running toward their own lines. Mickey figures the chase is on and he runs as fast as he can behind Sergeant Denman and Corporal Hadley holding his shotgun at hip level as he runs. He sees David and James within a few feet. All the rebel soldiers are screaming at the top of their lungs as they run.

Mickey is running as fast as he can and his obsession returns with a vengeance. He imagines himself singlehandedly engaging a line of Union soldiers and firing and bayoneting in a furious display of courage and fighting prowess. In reality it's only the backs of retreating blue uniforms.

Bzzz! Sounds like a bee going past Mickey, and he sees part of his left sleeve rip off, but he keeps running. The rebel charge reaches the group of Union soldiers mowed down by the big guns, and they jump and dodge around the motionless bodies on the ground. There's not a thought in Mickey except to get to someone in blue to shoot or stick with his bayonet, or both. His focus is laser-clear, and he feels neither fear nor hesitation. His adrenaline is coursing through every fiber of his young body. There's a puff of smoke ahead and several of those buzzing sounds, but Mickey runs forward. He can now clearly see horses pulling the union's big guns. They're in retreat up the little hill beyond the trees.

Many of the rebel infantry are screaming obscenities, the "rebel yell" and pausing to fire at the running Union soldiers.

"Run you blue bastards!"

Stand and fight ya chicken shits!"

"Yeeee ooh oooh!"

Mickey sees a puff of smoke ahead of the retreating soldiers and many of the buzzing sounds close by him. He quickly realizes it must have been a volley of shots trying to buy time for the blues to withdraw in retreat. Several of Mickey's company fall to the ground, but Mickey and Sergeant Denman are still running in the chase. Suddenly, Mickey hears a thundering behind him and more of the rebel yells. It's the rebel cavalry, swords drawn and forward charging past him.

Sergeant Denman stops and waves his arms. He turns to find himself only in the immediate company of his smallest, red-haired soldier- Mickey!

"Cease fire! Cease fire, Kid! Don't shoot our own cavalry."

Mickey stops running and realizes he's not fired a shot. Sergeant Denman is a few feet from Mickey, and so out of breath, he speaks haltingly, "It's cleanup time. Looks like for the moment we outran everybody else so let's head back toward the woods and regroup our company. On the way, help any of our guys you can but if it's in a blue uniform kick anybody who isn't blown apart. If they're faking it, disarm em and holler at me. We may take em prisoner. Don't take no chances. Don't let one of the fakers stab ya or shoot ya while ya think yer gonna take his gun. Be careful. If any doubt, stick em, and I mean, stick em good."

Mickey begins to follow Sergeant Denman's orders when the Sergeant addresses him, "Private, you okay?"

"Yes Sergeant. I'm fine."

"Well, tend to that arm when ya get back. You know I'm proud of ya. Yer one brave little red-headed shit. Helluva soldier!"

"Yes, Sergeant." Mickey looks first at his right arm and sees nothing amiss. When he looks at his left arm, it's blood-soaked from bicep area down to his wrist. It really stings. Mickey slowly rolls his sleeve up but can't see the wound. When he removes his shirt, he can see a wound about two inches long and maybe an eighth of an inch deep. It's bleeding, and Mickey knows he needs to take care of it because he's been warned not to get an infection from a lead bullet wound. Making his way back toward his own lines feels good. Mickey is empowered by his wound. He feels proud of being a wounded soldier- not a hero, just a soldier. Joe would be proud.

The next morning at assembly and roll call Mickey is one of five from all the companies singled out for bravery in battle. As Mickey and the other four face the eight-hundred or so of their comrades he cannot believe how he feels as all the soldiers are clapping giving the rebel yells. For Mickey it's like starving and then being fed a delicious meal.

After noon dinner, Mickey is sitting on a bench outside his tent talking with other soldiers. There's an air of camaraderie that was not felt before.

James takes a deep breath and spits behind where he's sitting, "Well, it's already turning out to be a better day than yesterday. I was really feeling scared when those first few shells came overhead."

"David laughs a little," When that happened, any man that says his ass didn't pucker is a liar."

Mickey chimes in,"Geez...what got me was when I heard that bugler and had no idea what we were supposed to do. Thank goodness I was close to Sergeant Denman otherwise I might have been the only Reb on the field chargin the Yanks. That might not go so good. "

"Hell, Irish, according to Denman this morning you by yourself mighta whipped em all alone."

They all laugh. It was only one skirmish in a big, big war but all the soldiers believe facing the sword yesterday makes them seasoned combat troops. Private John Weaver, who Mickey, David and James just met, is sitting on the end of the bench. Weaver laughs and points to a young man approaching them.

"This young guy comin down the way looks like he's from the other side of town. Way too much spit and polish to be down here with us grunts. Eh, Boys? Maybe he's lost."

"I don't know, John but maybe he's the general's pet pooch or something. I've heard they all have guys helpin em...ya know... the rich kids who are afraid to fight. Shit, this guy don't even look as old as Mickey."

They continue to stare as the young soldier occasionally stops to ask questions. And people point him on down the line of tents. He must be looking for someone. Then he pauses by the four sitting on the bench. "Pardon me, Gentlemen, but would you happen to know where I can find Private Michael Sean O'Day? He goes by the name Mickey."

Everyone on the bench except Mickey laughs. David squints at the young soldier, "This little red-head on the end is Mickey. What's he done now? Maybe ya gonna promote him to Sergeant or somethin?"

"Private O'Day. You are to accompany me to brigade headquarters. You need to be in uniform so I'll wait here while you put on your shirt and cap. If you need to take a minute to clean your boots that's fine, but we need to get back soon, and you need to be as presentable as you can be. Get a move on. The head shed's waiting on us."

Mickey stands up from his seat on the bench. He's more frightened than the battle yesterday. "What's this about? Something wrong? My brother, Joe…is he okay?"

"Private, I was sent to retrieve you to the Adjutant's office, Major Steines. That's all I know. C'mon, Private. Get ready, so we can get going."

CHAPTER 8

MOVIN' ON

At the Adjutant's office, Mickey feels out of place. Soldiers are busily hurrying about, each with a handful of what must be very important papers. It's apparent that to belong in the headquarters one must have polished boots, uniforms that fit and an air of superiority and confidence. At this point, Mickey has none of those and his confidence is gone.

A major crosses the room headed for Mickey. He appears to be in his early twenties and this is the first officer Mickey's met since officially being in the army. The major appears to be pleasant enough, "Private, O'Day? I'm Major Steines. This has been a good day for you I trust?"

Mickey pops to a rigid attention. "Yes, Sir."

"Well, you'll just wait right here for a couple minutes until the General is ready for you and then I'll take you in. You must personally know Colonel Maxwell. He's in with General Coates giving him some background on you." The Major pauses and then looks Mickey up and down, "Just stand at ease and have a seat. I'm curious, Private...how old are you?"

"Eighteen, Sir."

"Yeah. In a pig's eye you are. Well, anyhow, just have a seat."

Mickey's mind is racing. Colonel Maxwell inside that room must be the same Colonel Maxwell that was

Preacher Yount and the same Colonel Maxwell who signed Mickey up illegally. Mickey mouths to himself, "Shit. Hope the Colonel isn't in trouble for signing me up. What if I get booted out?"

The door to General Coates' office opens, and before the Major can rise, Colonel Maxwell is out the door, a big smile on his face, "Private O'Day. Good to see you again, Son. A little time and experience since we first met, huh?"

"Yes, Sir, Colonel, Sir."

Colonel Maxwell motions for Mickey to come to him. He shakes Mickey's hand and then points toward the General sitting behind a huge desk. Mickey reports in military style to the general.

"Sir...General Coates, Sir... Private Michael Sean O'Day...Company B...Regim…"

General Coates interrupts Mickey's litany of his chain of command and in a refined Southern voice, "Fine, fine...son how old are you or should I not be askin that, Billy?"

Colonel Maxwell smiles, "Sir, I brought this young man personally to the CSA. His older brother is already quite a legend, and I believe we have a second hero on a fast pace to do the same."

"Okay, Billy. I guess since you changed the subject we'll leave the age thing out of it."

Mickey can hardly believe his ears. He's soon to be sixteen years old and already described as an almost hero. It certainly doesn't seem that Colonel Maxwell or Mickey will be in trouble for being a little light on chronological years on this earth.

The Colonel continues, "General Coates, I am recommending we get Private O'Day assigned to one of our special units of our army. In fact, I'd like to get him in the same unit with his brother, Corporal Joe O'Day. That's Major Breault's Badger Unit. And Major Breault knows about Private O'Day"

The general immediately scowls and sits back in his chair, "Billy, you know we do not openly discuss or for that matter even acknowledge that unit." There's a pause, and General Coates continues," But you think this young man has the fight and fabric to be ready for...shall we just say, special duties? huh?"

"Yes, General. I believe he'll take to it like a fish to water."

"I don't need or want to ask you if you agree Private. You can't possibly know what special operations are about. I'll only say in many circumstances war is a very nasty business and sometimes we are called upon to do things that would be considered unthinkable in peacetime. Not every battle is fought on a field with artillery, cavalry and thousands of uniformed men. But if Billy Maxwell says you have the starch to be assigned to special operations, then I'll sign the orders and have the Adjutant get everything straight with your current regiment and company as well as your new one. You will be riding out of here within a day."

Mickey smiles a big freckle-faced smile, "Yes Sir, General Coates, Sir! I can do this I'm real sure. And I'm not squeamish about nothin. And besides…"

"Yeah, yeah, okay, alright, fine." The general gives a distracted half-smile and waves Mickey to leave, "Your dismissed. Do a good job. We're countin on ya, Son."

Mickey tries to do a military about-face, but the rug in front of the General's desk is way too thick. He twists his ankles stumbling a couple of steps but with hat in hand and not looking back Mickey quickly exits the general's office. Colonel Maxwell is a couple steps behind.

"Mickey, I'm going to write your Mama a letter and have the General sign it so she knows you and Joe will be together and how proud we are of your being a good soldier. Maybe it will keep her from being so mad at you and me when ya do get a chance to go home."

"Thank you, sir. Now, where should I go to get ready for all this changing of units?"

I want you to report right here to the Adjutant's office tomorrow morning when everybody in your area is havin breakfast. You get your stuff together and walk here without a word to anybody. By then Major Steines and his men will have figured out the details for all that has to be done to get you on your way. You'll likely be here all day. They'll cut you orders and escort you to the quartermaster to get you outfitted with some different uniforms and equipment. I think you'll be surprised and pleased. They'll collect what you have now and reissue it to somebody else. Tomorrow night you go back to your unit, but you don't know anything about what's taking place. Not a word. Understand? This is very secret. No hinting around that you're leaving or where you're going...or nothing like that...and I mean it. Just say you were called up to the Adjutant and you are pulled from your unit until your age is verified. They'll certainly all believe that."

"Yes sir, Colonel, sir. You can count on me."

The next morning holds more excitement than Mickey had imagined.

Mickey reports to Major Steines, "Sir, Private Michael Sean O'Day reporting as ordered."

"Good morning Private and I understand from Colonel Maxwell that you go by Mickey. That right?"

"Yes, Sir. Mickey's just fine...whatever you prefer, Sir."

Major Steines has three of his sergeants standing by his desk, "Then Mickey it is. Now stand at ease and as I explain what all takes place today, please be sure you understand and if you don't, just interrupt and ask. Okay?"

"Yes, Sir. I will."
"Okay, Mickey, you're going to get a lot thrown at you today. You'll get very little paperwork official and

otherwise. That way when you leave the post and in the unlikely event you get captured, or worse, your destination is not revealed. But my staff is going to give you lots of verbal instructions and passwords and the like. You commit that to memory, and we're going to be sure you know it before we let loose of you. Okay?"

"Yes, Sir. I'll listen real close, so I don't waste nobody's time."

"Your written orders are already dispatched by courier this morning. A copy to Regiment and a copy to your new unit. Dan here is going to take you in that room over there and go over the map of how to get to your destination. You will get a very crude copy of the map, but there's no way anybody else could know from that map where you're headed unless you tell them. Which you will not…right? You are not to mark anywhere on the map the route you are following. Your new special operations unit is about a hundred miles away from Camp Davidson and very close to the Arkansas-Missouri-Tennessee juncture and within twenty miles of the Mississippi River. The main headquarters of your new unit is at a Mississippi Island near New Madrid, but you're not going there. You are to join your unit directly in its secret location. After you're clear with the map, Phillip here will give you a series of passwords. They are never written down so you must memorize them and then pass a verbal test by Phillip later today."

After a grueling morning studying the map and getting verbal instructions and passwords, Mickey is accompanied to the quartermaster, and the experience is a thousand percent different than when he first arrived at Camp Whitespring upon enlistment. This time his uniform pants are fitted, and he's given a pair of shiny black cavalry boots. He's also given a utility uniform, a bedroll and some ragtag civilian clothes that he's to take along to the new unit.

The biggest surprises are when he's issued a sword, a rifle, a handgun and an eight-inch knife that fits in a scabbard on his right boot. Mickey is overwhelmed by the quality and quantity of what he's receiving, and he whispers to the Corporal behind the counter, "Wow. I thought only officers and sergeants received this kind of equipment."

The Quartermaster Corporal, with obvious and sincere envy of Mickey, says, "You get all the extra equipment cause you got hand-picked for a special unit. Most guys refer to the unit I suspect you're goin as the Badger Unit cause of the top sarge. Top, Top secret stuff but I know cause I got checked out real good to get this job. Them guys and your new outfit cause more fear in the enemy than the whole rest of the rebel army. They strike without warning and take no prisoners. I'd say you're damn lucky. Yep, pretty lucky. Hell, I'd say you must be some good fighter to get this assignment. Good luck to ya, Private. We're all proud to serve with the likes of ya."

By day's end, darkness is beginning to settle on the camp, and Major Steines gives Mickey a final once-over.

"Alright, Mickey, you've got all your equipment, and I want you to show it to me. Lay it out and say the name of each item."

Mickey complies.

"Now give me the password."

Mickey responds, "I don't know of any password."

"Then why are you on this trail?"

"Mickey responds, "I heard there's badgers around here and I like huntin badgers."

Major Steines smiles, "Good boy. You'll do fine. Stay out of sight, both from our guys and from the blue-bellies. You just stay on course to get to your assignment. You've got a hard ride but don't kill your horse trying to overdo it."

Mickey looks up at Major Steines, "What do I do for a horse? Do I borrow one from here?"

Major Steines laughs, "Mickey, you see that chestnut tied up over there? That's Chigger, and as of now, he's part of your equipment. He still belongs to the CSA, but until war's end, he's yours. He's a great horse, and I'm sure you'll love him. Colonel Maxwell said you're good with horses and to get you one of the best we have. Well, there he stands waiting for you. Go ahead and get acquainted."

"Jesus, Mary, and Joseph, Sir. That's a beautiful horse. Do I have your permission to bring him over here?"

Of course. Go get your horse. You take care of him from here on. And by the way, I don't want you to even go back by your old unit tonight. I want you on your way out of here. Go by the mess tent and get some cornbread and carry lots of water. As of this moment, you're dismissed from this regiment, and your assignment is to get to your new unit. Good luck soldier."

Mickey salutes, "Major, as soon as I gather up this gear and get some cornbread, I'm loadin up Chigger, and I'm leavin. I'll hide out sometime tomorrow and catch some sleep, but I'm ready to go."

The Major and the Sergeant look at each other and smile and then walk away. Mickey hears the sergeant say quietly to the major, "Sir, I wish we had a thousand Mickey O'Days. Good kid. Good soldier."

Mickey almost blows the buttons off his shirt when he overhears the sergeant. He's on the pathway to heroism and he feels it from the top of his red hair to the bottoms of his feet.

He continues packing, and within an hour he's outside of the camp. He passes two sentries as he leaves the area. They whistle the easily recognizable song of the whippoorwill and Mickey responds with four owl hoots. It works exactly as planned. After another two hours of riding, Mickey realizes he's way beyond any of the camp sentries. From now on it's time to watch his p's and q's.

It's a long night in the saddle, and Mickey stops where a creek runs close to the road. Chigger glistens in the light from a half moon and the Milky Way. He's a medium sized chestnut about fifteen hands at the front shoulder, a white blotch on his forehead, not anything close to a white star, and one ear is white on the inside.

"Ya know my friend, you could be in a herd, and you're so common nobody would notice ya. Chigger. I hope I can always keep you and do both cavalry and infantry. We'll make you a war horse, Chigger."

Mickey continues down the rutted buggy road and in the moonlight he figures he has traveled about eighteen miles of the hundred mile journey.

"Chigger, if we can do about twenty more miles or so. We'll take a proper rest. Then tomorrow eve we'll push a bit to get into our new camp the next day. Our camp, Chigger. Ya know bein out here alone in the night I feel so good. I love night. I'm not tired. I have a job to do. Get to camp. We just have to be careful."

Mickey slides off Chigger's back and walks him with the reins. He stops, takes an apple from the saddle bag and gives it to Chigger who devours it like he hasn't eaten in a week.

"Wow! You're a hungry boy. I bet they didn't bother feeding you before they gave you to me. Well, we'll take care of that shortly. We'll walk a while, and we'll find a place to get a bit of food...not so much you get bloated...just a bit to keep your strength. When it gets daylight, I'll find us a place to hide so you can get that saddle off and rest. Then tomorrow afternoon or evening we'll push, Chigger. We'll get to camp and see Joey. You don't know him, but he's the best brother a guy can have. He would protect me with his life. Ya know, Chigger, I'll make that promise to you. You be my war-horse, and I'll take a blood pledge to give my life before yours."

Chigger looks at Mickey, eyes directly on Mickey's eyes.

"Dang, Chigger, you're scarin me. I think you know exactly what I said and you are looking into my, my ...soul to be sure I mean it. And I do, baby colt. I mean it."

Chigger throws his head and snorts.

Mickey stands quietly for a second, "Is this just because I'm tired out, and I think this horse understands? I don't think so. Why did I get Chigger of all the horses out there at camp? I'm sure they gave him to me because he's considered good, but I think it was meant to be."

Mickey mounts Chigger, and they do a quick walk on down the road, Mickey keeping his eyes and ears open.

They move on for some time, and the moon is way over in the sky. Mickey tries to look at the map, and it's too dark for his fatigued eyes to see any detail. Mickey knows there's supposed to be a bridge at approximately the forty mile point and for sure they haven't reached that yet. Maybe he's overestimated what he and Chigger can cover because it's at the bridge that they leave the road and take off over land in a diagonal direction until they hit another buggy road. It's at the bridge there are frequent Union patrols. Time to be careful.

The first signs of a lighter sky seem to begin to the East, Mickey's right side' "Ah, the sun's still hidin but in an hour and a half or so it'll come up. And whaddayaknow, Chigger old boy, I think I see the outline of the bridge way up ahead. That's about perfect. We sure as hell don't want to be on this road in daylight. Liable to get snagged."

Suddenly without warning the bushes beside the road rustle and a man steps in front of Mickey and Chigger. The man holds a rifle at his waist, and it's pointed at Mickey. Even with the darkness, Mickey knows this guy is wearing a rumpled Union uniform, and the rifle is waving back and forth, up and down. Mickey puts his hands up, and Chigger comes to a quiet stop.

The soldier mumbles so much Mickey can barely make out the words. He must be drunk. Very drunk. Yet he's a big guy. He must be a full head taller than Mickey and outweigh him three times over.

"Yer, my prisoner! Haaak." The soldier gags and spits, "I'm guardin here. This my bridge up yonder. To guard. Less I say so, nobody comes through. You a Reb? Or who the hell are ya? Who'd think ye ar...?King of English or Americer?"

Mickey slides down from Chigger and puts one hand on Chigger's muzzle, his other hand in the air, "Stay, Chigger."

The soldier staggers a couple steps toward Mickey as he tries to focus, "Prisoner. No move or I kill ya. You a reb?"

"Nah, jest passin through. Beautiful night." Mickey slowly moves toward the soldier, and he's measuring to see if he can get close enough to take the gun away.

"Passin through. Everybody says that. I tell ya what. You don't look worth it to take prisoner, so I'm gonna take that horse of your'n as a toll to let you cross my bridge. Then you can walk wherever the hell yer a goin, and I can ride that broken down nag of your'n. "

Mickey's mid-section is just inches from the wavering bayonet, and now he's set to make his move, "Aw, you don't want that horse do ya?"

The soldier diverts his attention for a moment toward the horse, and Mickey grabs the barrel of the gun, shoving it straight up, and with his right hand, he hits the drunk square on the nose. The man staggers backward, stumbles and lands in a sitting position, totally dazed. Mickey's instinct kicks in and he wheels the gun around and jabs the seated man in the chest, rotating the bayonet, so it comes out cleanly. He jabs again and again. No resistance. There's a low, gurgling sound and Mickey can see in the moonlight blood is pouring from the soldier's mouth and his chest wounds.

"Done for, old timer. Just like Groundsie taught us...picture somebody and for you I pictured Sarge, the schoolmaster. Blue-bellies gotta be pretty hard up to put an old drunk like you out here to play sentry."

Mickey goes back to the patiently waiting Chigger and pulls his sword from the saddle scabbard. Mickey feels the edge of the sword to see how sharp it is and mutters, "It'll do just fine."

Mickey takes the soldier's uniform cap, ammunition pouch and he's already secured the rifle by tying it with a length of cord to his saddle holster. He stands for a moment and whispers, "Well, old-timer, guess I better get going. Wastin time stopped here, and this is where I leave the road anyhow. Nice meeting ya and I hope you don't have any need of this."

Mickey makes a quick slice with the sword and cleanly cuts off one ear of the dead soldier. He shakes some of the blood off of the ear, rolls it up in the Yankee's cap, takes his souvenirs and packs them in his saddlebags. Mickey returns and struggles from fatigue as well as the mismatch in size as he drags the soldier off the road into some weeds. He tries his best to kick dirt over the blood on the dirt road but can't tell how effective his cover job is going to be. Mickey shrugs his shoulders and thinks how easy it was to assess what he needed to do and then not just punch, but kill the Union soldier ala Corporal Ground's style. Maybe one day he'll meet up with Corporal Grounds and be able to tell him. But now is the time to get moving, so Mickey mounts Chigger and heads off the left side of the road, leaving his nighttime encounter behind. Mickey sits erect in the saddle thinking how proud he is to be so brave and such a quickly tested soldier. Boy, will Joe be surprised at his little brother.

As the darkness of night begins to get its first silvery light of the new day, Mickey sees the wisdom in being off the road. It's simple enough to head in a northeasterly direction, and he is out in the middle of woods and hills, hills and woods and woods and hills. Mickey's map doesn't show any farms or roads or even paths where Mickey is traveling. He seems to be right on track with the map and as instructed he's following a limestone bluff until he reaches Spellman Creek. He's to travel in the creek bed as much as possible for the first mile or so and then keep following the creek until he sees Piney Springs which is hard to miss. Even though there are no markings on Mickey's map he remembers the clear warning about the springs. He's not to hang around the spring too long because it is a well-known source of fresh water and very likely marked on Yankee as well as Confederate maps. Though the spring is a few miles from occupied properties, there is an ever-present possibility of stumbling upon a Yankee patrol or bunch of deserters, and that makes it a dangerous spot. After getting to the spring and the possibility of a quick drink for Chigger, Mickey is to go overland again, staying the northeasterly course until he intersects the Sparks Road. He'll have to look carefully because the Sparks Road is little more than lightly traveled wagon wheel tracks in the grass. At that point, he'll be about ten miles from his new camp, and he was instructed to just stay on the road until he's challenged by a sentry from his new unit. Just thinking about it makes Mickey's heart rate pick up speed.

In the meantime, he finds an overhang on the limestone bluff next to where he's riding, and though it offers little physical protection it looks like a perfect spot to get some much-needed rest for horse and rider. He takes the saddle and bridle off of Chigger and puts a rope loosely around his neck so he can graze within a few yards of Mickey's bedroll. Mickey unrolls his bedroll and quickly falls asleep from exhaustion.

As the sun gets toward noon, the light and heat of the sun wake Mickey, and he quickly looks around to see if everything is undisturbed. Everything appears fine. He breathes a sigh of relief because he was so sound asleep he may never have awakened if someone had entered his little campsite. He should never have taken a chance like that but his lack of true experience pushed his physical ability too far, and then he lucked out in getting some recuperation.

Mickey studies his map and figures he and Chigger spent about twelve or thirteen hours traveling last night including the ten or fifteen minutes he spent with the Yankee soldier. Mickey knows horses can cover about a mile in a quarter hour or roughly four miles in an hour but Mickey figures from the map he and Chigger didn't make the halfway point of fifty miles. He can't be certain until he intersects Spellman Creek but Mickey's anxious to get started again and allow Chigger more of a drink than the occasional rainwater pools along the bluff.

By afternoon Mickey and Chigger come to the creek and they rest there a half hour before moving on by slowly walking in the creek bed. Mickey isn't certain how far he's gone along Spellman Creek, but the sun is starting to get low in the western sky when he spots the big Piney Spring just ahead. Layers of mossy rocks and vegetation around the spring make it clear even from a distance. Mickey stops and looks carefully. Cautiously he lets Chigger wade and drink his fill. Then Mickey takes a bearing once again in the general direction of the Sparks road and his destination.

Mickey finds Sparks Road without trouble, and the moon is high in the sky. It seems almost daylight in the bright moonlight.

Mickey and Chigger travel along for several long hours when he is suddenly confronted by two armed men, "Down off that horse. Nice and easy and keep those hands in the air."

Mickey complies, holding Chigger's reins in one hand above his head. One man has his gun aimed directly at Mickey's head.

The other man comes closer. "Where ya headed?"

Mickey hopes these are two soldiers from his new camp. Otherwise, he has no idea what will happen. What if they're deserters and rob him or kill him? He nervously responds, "Heading North of here. Up the Mississippi."

"At least those look like the right uniform pants. So are ya lookin for your unit or runnin away from it? The only one near here is at New Madrid. That's fifty miles northeast of here, and you're heading northwest. I'd say you're lyin and think we're stupid. Whatdaya think? Hmmm?"

Mickey isn't quite sure what to do, and he squirms a little.

One man warns Mickey with the obvious click of cocking his rifle, "Stop twistin around like yer gonna run. You wouldn't do that would ya?"

Mickey bristles a bit, "No I ain't gonna run. I ain't no coward. I don't run away. I'm a soldier in the army of the Confederate States of America. My name is Michael Sean O'Day."

"Well, it sounds like we better quit messin with Michael Sean O'Day, Josh. Sounds like he's feelin a little scrappy. Ok then, soldier, what's the password?

Mickey smiles and takes a deep breath, "I don't know any password."

"Then what the hell ya doin out here?"

"I heard there's badgers around here and I like huntin badgers."

"Then Michael Sean O'Day, it is a badger you shall meet tonight and welcome to ya." Both men lower their guns, advance and shake hands with Mickey.

"So Josh will stay here, and I'll go get my horse to take you the rest of the way. Damn, now we have two O'Days. How we gonna keep em straight?"

"Cause my brother Joe is bigger than me, and he's a corporal."

"Jeezus Christ! Hear that, Josh? We got us Joe's brother! Man alive the Maj and Badger are gonna be lickin their chops for more action now."

The two ride into the forest and with the forest canopy shielding the moonlight, Mickey cannot tell anything about where they are going or how long this will take.

"Just curious but about how long will it take us? I'll be glad to get out of this saddle for a while and get some sleep."

"About another fifteen minutes we'll be there. By the way, I'm Chris. Chris Mayer. Actually, Corporal Chris Mayer but you're gonna find out quick that Sergeants and above are called by their rank. Otherwise, the rest of us are on name basis. You go by Michael?"

"Nah, just Mickey. So who's the Maj and this Badger fellow?"

You'll meet them soon enough. Major Breault is our commander. He's one tough coon-ass straight outa them bayous. When ya see his name written down it looks funny but don't worry none about how the major spells his name or what it looks like. It's pronounced like "bear" and "oh"...bear-oh. He's so smart it's scary. He ain't afeared of nothin or nobody...and he can back it up. He's Cajun and with a knife he can carve a man like a goose ready for the pan. Nuff said about the Maj.

Badger is the top sarge and the only human close to the Maj. Badger and the Maj plan every raid we do...and when they give the instructions for the raid and who does what, it gets done exactly like they say. My advice to you, Mickey-boy is answer them only when spoken to but don't get yourself in front of either one of them any more than necessary. I guess I love them as leaders, but they are definitely worth fearin, too. There's a downright mean streak in the two of em that runs all the way to the marrow of the bone."

"Okay, thanks for tellin me about them. Gosh, I can hardly wait to see Joe. I hope he's still awake."

"If Joe doesn't know you're comin then he's probably sleepin. There's a raid comin up either tomorrow night or the next. Depends on the clouds and moonlight. Badger named who's goin, and Joe is one of em on this operation. Nobody knows the details yet except it will be an all-nighter. Once the Maj and Badger get to see you in action a couple of times, you'll be gettin your fair share of our action."

They plod on silently for the rest of the way to camp, and occasionally Mickey notices Chris pauses his horse, leans way forward in the saddle and enthusiastically pats his horse's neck the same way every time. He leans forward and pats his horse's neck three times on the right, then two times on the left, and as he's sitting back up in the saddle, he pats him once more on the right. Three, two, one. Must be a silent passcode.

When they first reach the camp clearing Mickey can barely make out the size of the camp or even how many tents. There's one big campfire about fifty feet in front of what is perhaps the biggest tent. There's light flickering from inside the big tent, but the rest of the camp seems very quiet.

"Gee, Chris. Looks like almost everybody's sleepin. Seems like somebody could creep up on the place."

"You'll know all the signals soon enough. Comin in here to camp we went past three wide-awake sentries, and I guarantee they all know me personally, but you were with me so they had to challenge and I had to respond in order for us to get past them. Nope, this camp is armed and protected to the teeth. And ya don't see no Christmas trees of rifles stacked out front do ya? That's cause each man sleeps with all his weapons. Sleepin like babies at the moment and trustin our sentries but it would be a sad day for any bunch of blue-bellies who might think they can take us by surprise."

As the two horses draw close to the campfire, Chris indicates for Mickey to get down from Chigger. Chris hands Mickey the reins of his horse and heads directly to the lighted tent. The tent flap pulls back, and two men come out and join Chris. Mickey can't make out what they're saying, but all three turn and look Mickey's direction. Chris comes back over and takes both sets of reins.

"The Maj and Badger want to meet ya, Mickey. You be sure to report to the Maj properly with a salute."

Mickey whispers to Chris, "Which one's which?"

Chris laughs, "Oh yeah, you'd have no way of knowin. The skinny little guy with shiney boots is Major Breault. Badger's the big ugly sum-bitch next to him."

Mickey quickly reaches for his uniform cap from his saddlebag and when he does the union cap with the ear in it falls on the ground. Mickey looks at it for a second but leaves it and walks directly over to the tent.

"Major Breault, Private Michael Sean O'Day reporting for duty."

The major returns Mickey's salute and eyes him up and down. The intensity of Breault's eyes and his cold, unfriendly almost corpse-like face are captivating. It's as if he can see right through Mickey and there's not any reaction to what he sees. Breault is clean shaven, and his head isn't shaved but very close-cropped. He has a pretty face, almost feminine but Mickey's sure no one's ever told him that.

Mickey looks him in the eyes and in the dim light of the campfire, the major's eyes look pale and expressionless. He's maybe five feet seven inches or so, but he has a natural aura of authority. The major is wearing a white long-sleeve underwear shirt, tight cavalry pants, shiny black leather suspenders, and shiny black boots. Mickey wonders if Chris' description of the major was inflated.

It must be Badger who's the tough one. Now he's a big brute. He's even taller and bigger in every way than good old Corporal Grounds.

Badger has shaggy hair, he's sweating through his undershirt, and his uniform pants look like he slept in them. It seems odd but as unkempt as Badger appears his boots are like the major's, shiny as a mirror. Badger is smiling or perhaps smirking as his dark eyes pierce every inch of Mickey.

Major Breault nods his head in the direction of Mickey's souvenir, the union cap on the ground, "Looks like you dropped something soldier. Has a sort of Yankee look to it. Maybe you better bring it over here where I can see what it is."

Mickey seems frozen by the two leaders giving him a visual inspection, and as he hesitates for an instant the major steps toward him and puts his face only a few inches from Mickey's, "Son, you don't know me, but I'm gonna give you some advice. You should already be standin here in front of me holding whatever that is. When I say for you to do something, you jump…"

Mickey whirls away before the major's last word is out, he grabs the cap folded around the ear and hustles back to the major. Breault looks at the hat Mickey is holding and then smiles.

"I already take it we don't have to repeat lessons for this young man, Badger. Now tell me why you have a Yankee uniform cap in your saddlebag."

"Sir I took it as a souvenir yesterday from a sentry at the bridge where I left the road for the springs and then here. I killed him. And Sir, one of his ears is wrapped in the cap. I…"

So you killed a union sentry and took a little snack to chew on if ya got hungry?"

"Well, Sir, I…"

How old are you, O'Day?

"Sir, I…"

"Hold it! I actually don't want you to answer that question. Lesson two. Don't you ***ever*** lie to me. It's my job to know everything that goes on, but it is also my job to know that some questions are best if never asked. Your job, your only job is to listen carefully when I speak to you and do exactly what I say...and do not ever, ever lie to me. We clear?"

"Yes, Sir."

"Ya know, O'Day, I knew of you coming here yesterday. Colonel Billy Maxwell sent me word you'd be here as soon as he could get it greased with your commander. He's a man I trust. I also know and trust my very own Corporal Joe O'Day. A top soldier. I assume you're cut from the same cloth."

The major continues, "Chris will find you a place to sleep and something to eat if you're hungry. Tomorrow you'll get settled and have a chance to talk to Joe. For now, I welcome you and your little trophies. You certainly don't need to hide them in this camp. You'll see lots of little treasures you've likely never seen before. Okay, that's enough for now. You're gonna fit in just fine here. Dismissed."

Mickey salutes, and for his second attempt at an about-face he gets it just right and walks back to Chris. Chris gets the horses settled, and Mickey bunks in an empty tent for the night. His new unit. In the war with Joe. Everything is coming true. He falls asleep as soon as he rolls in his blanket.

CHAPTER 9

SETTLING IN…FOR ACTION

The camp comes alive at daylight. There's no bugler and no reveille to alert the sound sleepers, but everyone in camp stirs and talk to others who may still be in their bedrolls. Mickey slept soundly, and now he's wide awake, excited and refreshed. Maybe now he'll get to see Joe. As Mickey pulls back the flap of his tent and momentarily gets blinded by the sudden cascade of light, he sees the recognizable outline of Joe reaching to open the tent flap.

"Well, Michael Sean, what do ya have to say for yourself? Left our Ma to fend fer herself so you could see what this fightin's all about. Give me a hug ya little shit before I come inside there and knock ya around a bit."

Mickey lunges into Joe's waiting arms and the two brothers embrace. A few of the soldiers close by clap in appreciation of the happenstance reunion. Mickey is fighting back tears, and he dares not speak yet for fear his voice will show his emotion. Eventually, Joe steps back from Mickey and ruffles Mickey's hair as big brothers sometimes do as a sign of affection.

"Let's go get some chow, Mick. We can talk for a while before I have to report to Badger."

Mickey still hasn't said anything, but he smiles through his tear-glistening eyes and nods in agreement. Along the way, Joe takes great pride in introducing his brother to every single soldier they meet along the way to the mess tent. Mickey knows that Joe is proud to have him here. Every introduction is nearly verbatim, the last one before the mess tent is not different, “Hey Lester, this is my brother Mickey. You’re gonna have to put up with two of us redheads now.”

Mickey and Joe move on to the mess tent where they get hot biscuits, fried pork belly, molasses, and coffee. They go sit under a tree away from the others.

“Gosh, Joe, I’ll never remember all them names. Everybody seems real friendly though. That’s the first I’ve seen of that since I joined up. I mean, I’ve met some nice people but some aren’t nice at all, and I felt like I had to always watch out and be ready to fight just to prove I belong.”

“You just hit on it, Mick. We depend on each other in this outfit. You know the guy next to ya, in front of ya and behind ya will stand with ya when the chips are down. But until a few days ago when the major got the word you was headed here, I had no idea you had run away and joined up. I spose I better not even ask how ya got past the age thing, you lyin little mutt.”

“Nope, best not ask too much. Like the Maj told me last night. He’ll not try to trip me up with any questions where I might have to make up something. He scared me shitless with his speech on tellin him the truth. I suppose maybe it’s happened to somebody and they probably had to get a whooping by that big Badger.”

“Mick, you don’t know the half of it. The Maj is the tough one. Nasty, nasty, cold little man. He’s really smart, but he's also very scary… mean and cold. And yes there have been a couple of guys who he found had crossed him on one of our operations. The Maj took care of them personally." Joe draws his hand across his throat. "Mick, you'll get some trainin the next few days. Real special stuff. Pay attention. You shouldn't have no cause to have any talkin with the Maj or Badger. And when you're new, that's a good way to keep it. Learn all ya can. We do special jobs and in special ways. This unit doesn't stand in a line and shoot little lead balls at guys in blue uniforms. We are assigned some rough stuff and we often leave a real mess of people and things. You'll have to get your mind around that stuff. You'll find out. I know you can handle it. Yer a tough little shit and I'm mad at ya fer leavin Ma and the kids, but I'm mighty proud to see ya here. Mighty proud."

"I can't tell you how I've missed being with you, Joe. All I could think about these past few weeks is fightin along side of you, and maybe we'll be known as…"

"Don't talk like that. The hero stuff is usually on top of the last shovel of dirt when yer buried. That ain't my idea of feelin good. We'll do fine, and we'll survive this war so we can go home in one piece but promise me ya won't think about being no hero."

"Sure, Joey."

"Don't call me Joey. We ain't kids playin war. This ***is*** war. You're my brother Michael, or Mickey as you want, and I'm Joe or Corporal if yer in front of the Maj or Badger. Okay?"

Mickey leans close and whispers, “Sure Joey-boy. Got it.”

Joe punches Mickey in the shoulder and laughs, “I gotta go now. I’m gettin ready for a raid tonight. I may not see ya every day. You’ll be trainin. Pay attention. It ain’t like no fightin you ever seen before. But it’s what make us the best. Pretty soon you’ll get picked for some stuff...at first just to test ya out but then the real stuff...stuff you’ve never dreamed of...and I ain’t shittin ya, Mick. The excitement never stops.”

Joe tosses the rest of his coffee and stands up. He takes Mickey’s hand and begins to pull him to his feet but let’s go and Mickey falls backward and sits down hard. Joe leans down and whispers, “That’s from your Joey-boy.”

As Mickey walks toward the mess tent with the plates and tin cups from their breakfast, Chris joins him, “Morning, Mickey. Sleep good?”

“Yeah. I hardly laid down and I was knocked out. I was a lot more tired than I thought.”

“I see you, and Joe got to talk a bit. You may not see him anymore today. Depends on what they got planned. But I ain’t goin on this raid, so you’re assigned to me today, and I’m supposed to do trainin with ya today. Meet me here in about quarter of an hour from now, and we’ll get started. “

“Okay, Chris. What do I need to bring with me?”

“Just yourself, Little Man. “

“Okay, then I’m ready right now, and I’ll try really hard to learn whatever you got.”

Chris smiles a big grin, “Atta Boy!”

Chris points a direction to Mickey and the two walk toward a structure, part wood siding, and part canvas. A soldier sitting nearby rises to his feet and looks squarely at Mickey and Chris. Mickey is surprised at the apparent age of this soldier. He must be fifty or sixty at least. He’s tall and very thin with a long neck and a gobbler’s sag under his chin. He’d be a fright to meet in the dark but his clean, sharp uniform is spotless.

“Hey Chris, is this the new man I heard about? Joe’s kid brother? Maybe new ***man*** overstates it a bit. Don’t need no razor issued I reckon. You shave yet, Joe’s little brother?”

Chris puts his hand on Mickey’s shoulder and responds, “Give it a rest, Heinie. This here’s the one and only Mickey O’Day. Mickey, this here’s Henry Dittmeyer but he ain’t called nothin cept Heinie.”

“Don’t mind my remarks kid. I’m just pickin at ya. Glad yer here. I know Badger and Major Breault, and I know you wouldn’t be here if you weren’t a tough son-of-a-bitch. Hand-picked we are. Every God-damned one of us. So, Mickey let me show ya the storehouse.”

Heinie opens the door, and as he steps inside, he slides down a section of the side wall letting the sun illuminate the contents. Mickey squints his eyes to see what’s here. Lots and lots of Yankee uniform parts, swords, and a few Yankee regimental flags.

Heinie turns toward Mickey, "Depending on the mission the Maj sets up, you may need to wear or take some of this stuff. Damned detestable if ya ask me. Makes me sick when I gotta wear this crap. First of all, it's Yankee and second of all, nothin in here did much good for the guy who had it before it came here."

"Do I need any of this for what I'm doing today or pullin guard duty?"

"Nah, today you just need to see this place and know we got stuff for everything the Maj might dream up. As far as guard duty, you'll get your turn at guard duty soon enough. We guard this camp from a distance, close in and inside. No member of this camp will ever be taken from this camp. Now, outside of the camp? Well, that's The Maj's world, and that's where we work our magic."

Mickey looks questioningly at first Heinie and then Chris, "Magic?"

Chris grins a little, "Sure kid. Magic. Ain't no magic shootin a canon or chargin out across a battlefield in daylight. Not that they aren't important...just not magic. Now cuttin somebody's goozler without makin a sound, convincin' somebody to tell all their traitorous secrets, wipin out a nest of spies...now that gets to be magic. You'll see. Okay, we need to move on."

Mickey realizes the night at the Hoenisch farm the raiders left convincing evidence, so everyone in the area thought it was a bunch of Yankee deserters. So that must be some of the sorts of raids they do out of this camp. Mickey suddenly has a strange feeling. Just a passing thought, but it brings a chill. Mickey isn't sure what he thought this special assignment would be. He just wanted to be with Joe and fight next to him. He dreamed of a reputation of the "fighting O'Days." When he was picked for this, the Colonel and the General talked about special operations and Mickey pictured so-called special operations as being exciting assignments like sneaking behind enemy lines, sabotage, blowing up a camp or armory.

Somehow the idea of night raids on farmers isn't his idea of heroism. Burning a barn or stealing needed supplies is one thing. Even killing in some cases is necessary. But Mickey can't bring himself to think of doing what was supposed to have happened to Mrs. Hoenisch. That makes him feel sick to think of it. Mickey thinks that perhaps he's dwelling too much on the Hoenisch incident and his new unit probably does a lot of special operations besides farm raids. Besides, he's sure Joe wouldn't be hanging around long if all this regiment did was like what happened to the Hoenisches.

Chris and Mickey walk to a clearing where Chris motions for Mickey to sit down and then proceeds to lay out the contents of the canvas bag he's been carrying. Chris discusses passwords and signals used around the camp and when on raids. Chris tells Mickey he'll be asking Mickey to repeat those passwords and recite the signals frequently.

"And for sure, Mickey, Badger is gonna surprise ya within the next couple of days. He'll surprise ya and get right in yer face and start askin about the passes and signals. Practice hard and get em memorized like second nature cause he'll make sure you know em before he lets you go on an assignment. And if ya freeze up when he's askin, or ya get something wrong, he'll kick yer ass in front of everybody. Don't worry about it...just get em burned in right here," as Chris points to his head."

Next, Chris goes over camouflage and techniques for moving silently for both day and night operations. Mickey again recalls the night at the Hoenisch farm when Jack Tolliver and Sergeant Casey headed toward him in the dark and suddenly disappeared but then surprising Mickey from behind. So many little things to learn and practice.

The final lesson of the day is centered on the use of knives. Chris shows Mickey how to throw a knife and directs him to practice. Mickey's goal is to be an expert at throwing accurately and deadly between five and ten feet.

"Okay kid, you have about two days to be one-hunnert percent on stickin this knife hard and accurate. Don't do no good to sneak up, throw a blade and hit a guy in the chest with the handle. Hunnert percent you can't do that. You also gotta be a hunnert percent on all the passwords and signals. Ain't nobody gonna watch over ya to get this done cause we got more to learn. But it's up to you to practice on yer own. Get off here by yerself when you and I ain't trainin and practice. Say them passwords out loud. Learn and practice those signals. Stick that knife!"

"Yes, Chris. I understand. And I won't let ya down."

"Atta boy, Laddie."

The next two days are like a whirlwind for Mickey. Except for meals he's with Chris all day and learning more and more hand-to-hand combat and killing skills. Once more, Mickey surprises Chris as he did Corporal Grounds with how he has natural instincts for fighting regardless of his small size. Toward the end of the third day, Badger and Major Breault come to observe Mickey and Chris. The Major stands several yards away, expressionless but staring intently. Badger walks over and addresses Chris. They turn a couple of times and look at Mickey and then Badger comes directly up to Mickey.

Badger's a hulk of a man, and he looks directly down into Mickey's face, "Kid, the closest Major Breault ever comes to a compliment is the withholding of punishment, but this is an exception. The Major thinks ya look pretty good out here. Chris tells us you're doin good. The Maj is goin back to his quarters in a minute, but you'll walk with me back to the camp. I want to be sure you know all the passes and signals. Candy-ass Chris already warned ya I'd be askin so don't act surprised. Let's walk, O'Day."

Mickey pops to attention, salutes in the direction of the Major and turns back to face Badger, "Yes, Sergeant."

Mickey passes Badger's questions with flying colors, and as they enter the center of camp, Badger stops and says to Mickey, "O'Day, I'm gonna recommend the Major include you in the guard roster and also a couple of small operations to see how ya do."

Badger doesn't wait for a reaction but just turns and walks away. Mickey feels relieved and is anxious to become a regular part of the camp and these so-called operations.

The next day Mickey is notified of several guard shifts over the next month, all midnight shifts and accompanying another experienced guard. Mickey soon realizes the midnight guard shifts are to get accustomed to expecting overnight activities and get the body used to different sleeping patterns.

Mickey is notified he'll be on a midweek raid and he and four others will be briefed the next day and then leave at first light the following day to get in place for their operation.

At the appointed time Mickey and three other soldiers meet outside Major Breault's tent. Mickey has met the other soldiers picked for this mission but struggles to remember all the names. They all shake hands with Mickey and reassure him they are glad to have him in this operation. Badger comes out and directs the four soldiers to a long wooden table with benches. Major Breault and Badger come to the table, put the soldiers at ease, and the entire group sits on the benches around the table.

Major Breault addresses the group, "Your Sergeant in charge on this operation is Sergeant Willis. He's already been briefed on this, and he'll review details with you along the way to the spot you'll set up. Now Badger will fill you in on the mission."

Major Breault, emphatically taps his finger at a spot on the map, nodding at Badger to begin. In his deep voice, Badger speaks without hesitation, "This operation is to steal a herd of approximately a hundred horses the Yankees are moving overland to Wagonite, Mississippi. The Yanks guard the town's railway station, and once there, it's safe for the horses to be transported east. They only got one thing wrong with their thinking...we're gonna steal those horses for our cavalry before they get to the town and rail station. Badger continues to lay out detail after detail. Each man is given a handmade map showing points of identification and distances as well as expected horseback time to the site of the rustle.

After a couple hours of Badger's briefing, the soldiers are released, and Mickey decides the best thing he can do is get some food and try to turn in early. May not be much sleeping for the next couple of days.

The next morning Sergeant Willis has all five horses waiting for their riders in front of Major Breault's tent. Mickey and the other men are a few minutes early and tend to the task of loading their horses. Sergeant Willis also has the pack mule for carrying coils and coils of rope. Not a lot of weight but quite a bulky load.

Major Breault steps from his tent and all the soldiers stand at attention in front of their respective horse. Major Breault looks them up and down and then quietly addresses them, "Men, I watched each of you listening to Badger yesterday, and I know you understand the importance of this mission. I want it done perfectly so think the details and listen to Sergeant Willis. I expect this to go exactly as the plan. Do the unit proud and I will listen for your return until you are safely back with your brothers in arms."

Major Breault abruptly turns and goes back inside his tent. Sergeant Willis gives a hand signal to mount, and then he leads the raiders at a slow walk from camp.

In the afternoon the small band of raiders are resting their horses, and Sergeant Willis begins to go over the details of their mission once again, " We know the rancher who sold the herd to the Yankees. He sent his own cowboys to deliver the horses, and they 've brought the herd from western Nebraska without any trouble. That's cause we secretly made sure nobody would cause them any trouble. We figure night after tomorrow, Wednesday, being the last night before they turn the herd over to the Yanks they'll be feelin pretty sure of themselves. We have been informed that the rancher's men intend to deliver the horses to Union soldiers about mid-day this Thursday and then blow off steam in town. We will simply relieve them of their responsibilities the night before. That's why we left at first light this morning to give us plenty of time to get in place and be ready to get this done. We'll arrive at our position late tonight and set up so tomorrow we can watch as the herd arrives and the wranglers get ready for what they think will be a peaceful night. Any questions so far?"

"No Sergeant," in unison.

Mickey listens intently to every detail, and he's excited that he gets to take part. He's confident with horses, so this seems a great opportunity.

Willis continues, "Okay, after the herd left Nebraska into Iowa we've had scouts watching since they entered Missouri out of Iowa, then East and now headed south, stayin along the Mississippi. We know the wranglers haven't had any trouble so far and they're over the jitters but they still go through the motions of guardin them horses. At night they keep their personal horses separate from the main herd, so it's absolutely critical we get the personal horses first. Don’t want even a ghost of a chance that somebody is able to escape. Got it?”

“Yes, Sergeant Willis.”

The Sergeant takes a deep breath, spits, “Our scouts report there are approximately a hundred horses in the herd and five cowboys, and they place one man to guard overnight. The one guard walks the perimeter of the camp which includes the cowboys’ horses and the herd enclosure. The night guard duty is on from approximately two hours after nightfall until about six in the morning. Between two and five in the morning, the guards begin to relax and don’t seem too anxious to continuously walk and usually get coffee from the campfire and then go sit close to the herd. We’ll get as close as possible to the wrangler’s camp around midnight, spot the guard and be certain the rest are in their bedrolls. You’ll have your handgun of course, but The Major doesn’t want no shootin on this operation. Nice sharp knives. Clean, quick and silent. The guard will be killed first, and then you’re to kill the remaining sleeping wranglers. Each of you will be assigned a wrangler to take care of. At that point, the horses will be rope-haltered. Each of youse grab ten horses and tie the rope halters to a master lead rope. There’s twenty knots in each rope, and ya gotta tie the halter rope in between two of the knots on the rope. As quick as they’re hitched you skedaddle due West outta camp. It’s about six miles from the horse camp to a little-known rail spur jest this side of Blue Point Crik, and our good old CSA cavalry will be awaitin. When you get close, you should see some train cars and our guys. You turn over them horses, and then you high-tail-it back to the campsite and then all five of us including me will get the last horses out. I'll keep haltering and tyin em to a stringer while you boys are gone with the first bunch.. The plan is to have all horses delivered to Blue Point Crik by daylight. Then we head back home to try to make the major and Badger smile. Anybody ever see that happen?"

Everyone laughs. "Shit, Sarge, if Badger laughed his lips would crack and bleed."

Willis laughs too and then continues, "Just so ya remember, once this starts ya gotta hurry it up cause it wouldn't be a complete surprise if a small Yankee escort party comes to meet the wranglers in the early morning to ride the final few miles to their railway station in town. If that happens and they find the remains of the camp some will go back to get help, and the rest will likely start to track the herd being moved west."

Willis takes a deep breath, spits and continues,"Our Cavalry will have snipers at the Blue Point Crik crossin in case some Yankees show up. The Cavalry intends to be quick about loadin the horses that are going South by train but they are takin some of the herd to pressing needs elsewhere."

The plan goes like clockwork at the appointed time. Sergeant Willis has each of the men in place while the wranglers situate the horses for the night. It seems obvious the wranglers assume this night will be like the others, uneventful. It's also obvious the wranglers assume this is the last night before some hooting and hollering in Wagonite. Eventually, nightfall finds the wranglers in their bedrolls and one sentry walking his post without much motivation.

Just as Sergeant Willis planned, the lone sentry is taken out with a knife to the throat. At Sergeant Willis' signal, Mickey descends to his slightly snoring, assigned bedroll. Without a second thought, he silently dispatches his wrangler target and rises to see that all the others have done the same. Willis checks each body and then speaks aloud, "Okay, Gents. Time to get to work rustling a hundred and five head of horse flesh. Get at it!"

Rounding up the horses and getting them rope chained together is quick and easy. Within a few hours, they are back for the final batch, and it all goes off without a hitch. Not a shot fired. Results are five dead wranglers, a hundred-five head of horses delivered, and the Yankees left in embarrassment.

Mickey, Sergeant Willis and the rest of the raiders return to their unit's camp between nine and ten Friday morning. They ride into camp and stop their horses in a straight line in front of Major Breault's tent. Sergeant Willis dismounts, walks to the front of the major's tent and knocks on the board covering the front tent pole. Major Breault comes to the flap, chats briefly with Sergeant Willis and then steps out of the tent. He walks with the Sergeant in front of each horse and rider, looking into each pair of eyes, horse, and rider as he walks the line. Without a word said or any expression he turns and walks back inside of his tent.

Sergeant Willis faces the four mounted horsemen, "Good job, men. The Maj is jumpin with joy as ya can see. Boys, I'm proud to serve with ya. Now yer dismissed and go get some chow and some rest."

With that, each man turns his horse and walks then toward the livery. As Mickey dismounts, he begins to take the bridle off his horse but hears over his shoulder, "Hey, Mickey, when you complete a mission you can go straight from here to the mess tent and then get some sleep. Here comes Walt to take care of the horses and let's go see what Cookie will whip up for the most recent heroes."

Mickey whispers to himself as he walks to the chow tent, "Heroes? Heroes? We murdered some guys who were asleep. They weren't even soldiers. We stole some horses and cut the throats of five innocent guys. We're heroes? Jesus, Mary, and Joseph, I gotta talk to Joe. I don't feel so good about this."

But first things first and Mickey craves food and sleep at the moment.

After refreshing with food and rest, Mickey lies on his cot feeling disillusioned. Are these the sort of big battles and important operations he's destined to do for the rest of the war? Sure, stealing horses for the CSA is important but Mickey's recollection of his first and only real battle, charging across the field with his sergeant, bullets sounding like bumble bees in a blackberry patch- now that's war. If only he and Joe could charge together across a field like that, shooting, bayonets at the ready. He never felt the slightest bit of sympathy for Yankees on that field but for some reason cutting a sleeping man's throat is not even close to the same. One is soldiering …combat. The other is murder.

Mickey continues to struggle with his feelings about his introduction to the reality of his new war. He's very frustrated, and he can never find a time where he can just sit down and simply talk to his big brother. It seems the more frustrated Mickey gets, the more he wants and needs to talk to Joe, but Joe is only seen from a distance. It's as if the two O'Day s are deliberately kept apart, and to Mickey's added suspicion it seems Joe does nothing to remedy the situation. Joe catches Mickey's eye and waves or winks but always seems to be in a hurry to rush off in the opposite direction from Mickey. Joe and Mickey are on the same guard shifts but in far different locations. When Mickey looks for Joe around the camp, Joe's either out of camp on a special project for Badger, or he's sleeping or preparing for an operation.

CHAPTER 10

VESTIGE OF INNOCENCE

A few days pass, and word is sent to Mickey that Badger has selected him for another special operation in two days. Joe is also selected for this operation. It sounds to Mickey like half the camp will be involved. Everyone assigned for this mission is instructed to gather in front of the Major's tent at five o'clock, right after chow. As soldiers assemble everyone seems to know what to do. People sit on the ground forming a circle with an open center about ten feet across. At five o'clock Badger comes out of the tent first and closely behind is Major Breault dressed in full uniform.

Major Breault speaks loud and clear, "Men, keep your seats. I'm going to explain the next mission of our unit."

Breault takes his place in the center of the circle, talking and walking, "The orders for this mission come from what is termed I-One. I-One is at the top of the CSA intelligence department and is in a secret location, but just between you and me I think it's located in Montgomery, Alabama near the home of our President, Jefferson Davis."

A few of the men laugh a little and the Major continues," The target is a huge, very successful farm owned and run by Oscar Blankenship, his family, and approximately fifty slaves. Mister Blankenship is very influential in the region and even made a bid for

Governor at some point. Apparently the Blankenships do not get all their wealth from tilling the soil. They are paid handsomely to house Union spies, keep a stockpile of both U.S. and CSA money on hand and store vast amounts of armament and equipment. The Blankenship farm is a suspected secret depot, so union troops are well supplied as they make forays into the southern states. That's our target. We will render the Blankenship farm useless and while we're at it we're going to get every shred of information from our guests. While we are there we'll relieve the Blankenships of all their money and all the arms we can haul away. This will severely cripple the Union's war effort. This is important!"

Major Breault is enjoying this and continues, "You'll see maps later but for now I'll explain some of the raid details. The Gasconade River runs through the Blankenship property, and CSA intelligence now knows there's a so-called secret cavern on the farm. It has an entrance in one of the river's limestone bluffs on the property. The cavern entrance on the bluff is some twenty feet up the side of the bluff and the entry about four feet high and wide and well-hidden with vegetation. The other end of the cavern and the main entrance is secreted in the large barn just a couple hundred feet from the main farm residence. Though this cavern has remained a secret, one of the Blankenship's slaves ran away and was luckily caught by a CSA detachment and turned over to CSA intelligence. The slave leveraged his way to freedom and provided details of the cave, number of guards and even some of the high ranking Union generals who have visited. Boys, this is a good one and we'll milk this Union cow dry.

A weakness of the secret is that the cavern is not usually guarded at the bluff entrance. but a small four-man detachment in civilian clothes guard the barn and daily walk the entire quarter-mile length of the cavern and look out of the opening in the bluff to be sure the tunnel isn't compromised. Our details tomorrow will tell you exact times, what each man will be assigned to do and how we achieve complete mission success. Now go talk about this and get some rest. We do the details tomorrow at five o'clock."

This sounds exciting to Mickey. Finally, something makes sense.

The final details of the operation are briefed the next day by both Major Breault and Badger. Both Mickey and Joe will be in this operation. Mickey smiles at Joe as the times, and specific assignments are ready to be given. This sounds really important, and Mickey and Joe will finally get to be shoulder-to-shoulder.

The circle of soldiers form again as they await the details from Badger and the major. Mickey squirms and his heart races in excitement.

Badger begins the briefing, "First, we will take complete control of everyone on the farm. Second, we'll interrogate to obtain any information that CSA intelligence can use and get all the money. Third, we'll take all horses and as many wagons that we need and use them for packing cow carcasses, armament and explosives. Fourth, we burn the buildings and blow up the cave so it can't be reopened."

Suddenly Major Breault laughs and wiggles his eyebrows. He actually smiles when he quietly says,

"Fifth and finally, Souvenirs and pleasure should be a plenty."

Mickey and the newer men all look around at each other. The old-timers of the camp immediately start catcalling, clapping and laughing. Major Breault holds up his hand. Silence is surgically quick, and he continues, "Oh yes, I have no reason to doubt our success so at my direction, when we are ready to leave, you can take anything you want for souvenirs and have all the fun you want. Just remember, when we leave there will be no escapees, no survivors and no remains of that God-damned Yankee depot. But one rule. When I say it's time to go, you button up, you burn it up, and you saddle up. Got it?"

There is a unison of, Yes, Sir." The men are clapping and laughing again. Excitement seems contagious except for Mickey. It sounded good at first, but he fails to understand the laughing and clapping about this last part. To Mickey, this operation is taking on the same characteristics as the horse raid and the Hoenisch farm. It sounds like murder and savage brutality for fun. As the major calls it "souvenirs and pleasure". Mickey is straddling the line between being a boy, a man, or a cold-blooded killer. He feels like he has no mental armor to do this without terrible guilt. The last vestiges of naivety and nervous innocence are escaping like wisps of smoke.

Badger picks up the briefing, "With all the pack horses and wagons we will be slow-going to get back here to safety so as we leave the farm we figure the first three or four hours we are very exposed to being spotted by a Yankee scout. We can't move fast or hide with wagons and pack horses. I don't care how tired ya are, I'll call out who goes two ahead, two behind and one drifter on each side of our merry band. And when it's yer turn to guard I better not catch anybody daydreamin."

Everybody nods and grunts acknowledgments but the Major looks over the group of men and continues, "This is very, very important. Each man must know exactly what to do and when. This is why you're trained. We don't have five-hundred stupid foot soldiers to attack this place and stumble around cause there's no battle line or sergeant telling em to charge. I will use sixty of the best raiders in military history. That's you!"

He pauses and makes direct eye contact with everyone he can and then continues," Get this right. The South needs heroes and legends to recruit and also to regain some of the pride taken away by the blue-bellies. We need heroes and legends to pry more soldiers away from their whiny little excuses and get em to feel some spirit to win this war. Okay. Take a fifteen-minute break and then get back here for your specific assignments. Fifteen minutes! Dismissed."

After the men return, Mickey looks at the group in the flickering firelight. It looks like more than half the soldiers in camp are going on this operation. Mickey's stomach is turning with excitement but a lot of trepidation. He cannot reconcile the feeling that charging into battle with his sergeant caused him no fear at all to kill an enemy soldier. He felt no remorse, just pure adrenaline when he killed the drunk soldier at the bridge and cut off his ear. He was glad that the Hoenisches were burned out and even murdered. But he has never allowed himself to picture in his mind what his school teacher meant when he said that unspeakable things were committed on Mrs. Hoenisch and even the torture committed on Mr.Hoenisch, Harry and Elmer. Mickey does not allow himself to think about how he blindly followed orders to kill when they nabbed the horses. He cut the throat of that unsuspecting wrangler rolled up and snoring in his bedroll. Murdering defenseless people for sure cannot be right by any stretch of the imagination.

Mickey's thoughts turn to Joe and how the infrequent letters to his Ma both from Joe and the CSA talked only about how proud Joe is to be on the side of right and honor. Joe's been in this unit long enough to know this sort of killing is neither right nor honorable. Mickey just finds it difficult to understand how Joe can square the actions.

Mickey stares at the faces of his fellow soldiers and is shocked that most are smiling with excitement and leaning forward in anticipation for the sound of their name so they can get their part in this horrible event. Joe has the same expression. When Badger calls out a name, the soldier stands, and Major Breault tells him exactly what he is required to do two nights from now. Once the major is finished with a man's assignment, there is a celebration of clapping and several crude comments until Badger reads the next name. These soldiers are very happy being told to commit torture and murder. Mickey secretly hopes his name will somehow not be called and he looks again at the celebratory expressions as each piece of this macabre event falls into place.

"O'Day? Michael." Badger reads from his ledger book.

There's silence as people around Mickey turn and look at him and one man even jabs him on the arm to get him to respond. Silence.

An irritated Badger growls, " O'Day! You deaf or asleep? Boy, I don't like bein disrespected. Get on yer feet and listen to every word the major tells you. You and I will have a little one-on-one time after this briefing to make sure you're payin proper heed."

Mickey rises to his feet and faces Major Breault. Badger's mention of one-on-one brings muttering under the breath from the soldiers around Mickey. He knows it's not good to get on the bad side of either the major or Badger and perhaps he's just accomplished both. Mickey's stomach feels like he's going to throw up, but he stands erect and tries to project a confident voice, "Yes, Sir Major. Private O'Day ready for orders."

The dark tan face of Major Breault has a crimson overtone to it, and he's obviously irritated, "Shut your mouth, kid. Your daydreamin wastes everybody's time. That's bad enough. But daydreamin or losing concentration during a mission can cost lives of your brother soldiers. That I would not forgive or show leniency. I think Badger will explain that in a little more detail after this is over. Now here's your assignments for day after tomorrow."

The major outlines exactly what Mickey is to do, has him come up and look closely at the map until he's convinced Mickey knows what to do and when. Mickey returns to his place and sits down. No one makes a sound. No celebration or pat on the back. People avoid making eye contact with Mickey. Mickey looks at Joe, and Joe stares directly into Mickey's eyes then turns his head away from Mickey and toward the major. Mickey's breathing is shallow and quick. He is really afraid and wonders if a one-on-one with Badger means a beating, a lecture or both. Well, if that's what it is, he'll take it like a man. Regardless of his serious misgivings about participating in these so-called special operations, Mickey doesn't want to get into trouble or get Joe in trouble.

The briefing carries on in detailed instructions. It is astounding to Mickey that Badger and Major Breault have such details prepared and committed to memory. The details are also recorded in ledger books. The two of them must spend every waking moment planning operations. As a group they are told what to wear and what to take. One of Mickey's assignments is to take six, fifty foot long coils of half-inch rope, six coils of one-inch rope and eight rope halters for pack horses. The men are told who carries what type of weapons, how much ammunition, who takes the dynamite, black powder, fuse, and blasting caps. Mickey's head is spinning with all the datails, but as he looks around at the other faces, most seem confident and have likely done this many times before. So for those with experience, it's more a reminder than a whole new list of details.

The major draws the briefing to a close, "Men, I'll say again how important this is to the entire war effort. We will meet on the field at first light tomorrow and walk through every single assignment. Know your parts. Rehearse them tonight in your mind. Enough for tonight. Dismissed."

As the major opens his tent flap and disappears inside, Badger stands staring at Mickey. Mickey stands and walks toward Badger and then stands at attention looking up into the face of the man that towers over him.

Badger growls in a whisper, “Kid, you ain’t no more important to me personally than a pecker gnat on a dog. I ain’t your ma or your brother. So, I don’t love ya, and shit’s truth I’m not even sure I like ya... but you are important for one reason, and that is you are part of this operation, and your brothers’ lives depend on you. That’s important to me, so you have to know your part and carry it out to the letter. Tomorrow you have to show you know your tasks and can carry them out. I’m cuttin ya some slack this time because of yer brother. Now get outta my sight and no more of this.”

Mickey is relieved but tries to only show his respect, so he salutes Badger, says, “Yes, Sergeant,” and does an about face and walks off toward his own tent. He can feel Badger’s eyes staring a hole of contempt through him. Tomorrow he’s got to put everything out of his mind and concentrate only on what’s expected of him. No more questioning what’s being done. That has to stop. Then he’ll talk to Joe and see if Joe thinks he can get a transfer back to his old unit.

True to the spirit of a final dress rehearsal, the morning walk through takes each group of soldiers and individuals within each group through their assignments for the next night’s Blankenship raid. Mickey is impressed how Badger and Major Breault know the details and timing so well the confidence grows throughout the day of practice. This raid has the makings of a particularly gruesome one because if done perfectly there will be few if any, gunshots. The big noise will be the blowing up of the cavern at the last, but even that will be muffled. Smoke from the burning buildings will likely be the alert to enemy forces...or so it is hoped.

For the remainder of the day, soldiers go to the various supply tents drawing what they need for the mission. Word spreads that assembly will be at six o'clock tomorrow morning. One pack animal from camp will have meat, bread, and water for some last minute energy before the "festivities" begin.

Tonight Mickey has trouble sleeping. He tosses and turns. First, he's too warm, then he's too cold. He knows he's very worried about participating in this not only from the point of gruesome murder but also his gnawing thoughts of how he can get reassigned from this brigade and rejoin his old unit without it reflecting poorly on Joe.

Finally, daylight arrives as a relief to the restless night, but for the next thirty-six hours Mickey must be at his best to avoid personal trouble and avoid making trouble for Joe. Mickey repeats over and over again moving his lips in the silent mantra, "Just do your job...just do your job...just do your job."

At first light, all the soldiers committed to the operation are on horseback, in a single long line in front of Major Breault's tent. One of the guards staying behind brings the saddled horses for the major and Badger. The tent flap opens, Badger steps out and holds the flap and Major Breault makes his appearance. The major looks like he should be on a recruiting poster. Every bit of silver and brass gleams, his boots are like glass and his sword sparkles. The major mounts his horse, Badger mounts his, and the two walk their horses to the far end of the line of soldiers. They proceed to walk slowly back along the entire line looking each man in the face. There's not a word spoken nor a change to the major's expressionless face. As they pass Mickey, his heart races as he suddenly has a feeling they will stop and single him out. But they approach and then pass with all the indifference being served to the other soldiers. As they near the final soldiers, Badger looks back over his shoulder, then turns straight in his saddle, raises his right arm and gives the signal and command to follow, "Column of two's...f'ward!". The line moves out in a long line, two-by-two. Not a word is spoken.

Later, as the afternoon turns to dusk and then into darkness, the column moves at a quicker pace and the two assigned sentries behind and in front make sure there will not be any unseen impedance to the plan. Well into darkness and the column leaves the road and moves to an open field on a hilltop. As Badger whistles, Mickey strains to see in the darkness, and he sees the silhouette of Badger's raised arm against the sky. Mickey supposes they must be close to the Blankenship property. The men dismount and quietly talk as the salty meat, bread and water are dispensed. What had not sounded very appetizing a few hours before now is an astonishing, welcome taste.

Word is passed to form a single line and position with group members of assigned tasks. As the line forms, small candles are passed along the line, "One candle and holder for each team."

The candle holders are pint size, open-top, tin cylinders. A lit candle sits inside the cylinder, and when the cylinder is twisted, an opening on the side of the cylinder exposes the candle light in one direction, The shiny inside makes the light focus brighter and only in one direction. The line begins to edge forward, and word is passed back the line, "All pocket watches out."

Mickey can make out the major and Badger ahead. The major has a white sheet on the ground, and it must be a map only a little bigger than the one he studied in camp. Now Mickey sees clearly what is happening. Badger is checking to make sure everyone has a pocket watch, and it's showing the correct time. Each group gathers at the edge of the sheet, and the candle holder is opened. The major points with his sword first in the direction of the farm below the hill and then to the map. His only instruction is, "The map on the ground is the same layout of the farm, and the directions are the same. Nod if you are ready." The major then looks at each man and every person nods. The candle is blown out after which candle and candle holder are left on the ground.

It's very quiet on the hillside, and most of the soldiers are sitting in groups just waiting for the word to proceed. At ten o'clock Badger walks throughout the troops and gives the word to walk horses toward the farm. Very quickly the soldiers and horses are making their way toward the farm. About three hundred yards from the closest building they are all halted, and every man is caring for his horse to be sure of quiet. The horses are all secured. Two men are sent to find the Yankee soldiers on night patrol, make sure it's only the usual two by making a quick pass around the outside of the buildings and then silently kill the guards. About twenty minutes passes and the two report back to the major. The soldiers now move forward to within a couple hundred feet of the house and barn, and the rest of the plan goes into action.

Mickey faces the farm buildings. They are exactly where the major's maps and drawings said they would be. The house is the building farthest to the left of the complex. Two-hundred feet to the right of the house is the building that looks like a big barn where inside is the large secret entrance to the cavern and upstairs in the building are quarters for a few other Yankee soldiers and any Union spies that may be temporarily staying in safety on the premises. A hundred feet to the right of that building and a hundred feet to the rear is the one long, single-story building for slave quarters. The corral and actual stables are behind the big barn and in front of the slave quarters.

Mickey's first job is to guard the outside west side of the farmhouse to be sure no one tries to escape. Mickey's three partners take up similar guard duty, one soldier on each side, one front and one back of the farmhouse. They are to do this until they are given the signal that the house and occupants are secured. Simultaneously the attack takes place to quickly control the entire farm. Ten soldiers get all the slaves out of their quarters and keep them in one group. Ten soldiers execute the sleeping Yankee soldiers as well as one other unidentified person on the second floor of the so-called barn. When that task is completed the ten in the barn move through the entire length of the cavern, being certain no one is there and taking a rough inventory of what arms and munitions are kept in a large cavern room near the barn entrance. If there happens to be anyone in the cave and they attempt to escape at the small bluff entrance, Major Breault has a soldier stationed below the opening as well.

Simultaneously ten soldiers quietly enter the house, two kill the house servants who live in first floor rooms. The other eight rush upstairs to each of the four bedrooms and roust Mr. and Mrs. Blankenship, their sixteen-year-old son, and their fifteen and twelve-year-old daughters. Mr. and Mrs. Blankenship are taken downstairs, separated from each other and separated from the children while they are interrogated personally by Major Breault.

The interrogation goal is to find the money, written plans or agreements with the Union army, and the details of the Blankenships' collaboration with the army. Of particular interest is to find out if there are more of these secret depot systems. Major Breault conducts the interrogation and Joe is to physically assist in convincing them to talk.

Jack Tolliver is one of the six to secure the barn and cavern, and Mickey sees Badger come outside to the front porch to talk to Jack. The barn and cavern are secured, the slaves are accounted for and secured, and Jack is giving Badger a rundown of what is available in the cave. Badger signals Mickey and the three other house guards to begin their next assignment to get to the corral and stable, get any serviceable wagons, horses to pull them, and get them around to the front of the cavern entrance. They are to then put rope halters on four horses destined for packing cattle carcasses back to camp.

Mickey's tasks are to be completed in an hour, but he finishes early and looks at his watch. It's not quite three in the morning. More soldiers complete their assignments and gravitate to the front of the farm house where some sit on the porch and others stand in small groups. Though the voices are not loud, there are a few smiles and congratulatory small talk.

Badger exits the front door and waves his right hand over his head in a circular motion to gather everyone in the general area. He motions again, "C'mon up here closer so I don't have to shout. We got a shitpot of money and some gold bars. The Yanks have been storin and passin money through here since this war began. Well, it's Jeff Davis' money now. The old man Blankenship was gonna be a hero and not tell nothin even when Joe mounted his old lady and made her pure Irish by injection. So we trotted him upstairs and let him see Jack about to bust cherries of his two little girls. He sang like a canary. The Major and Whitworth went to the hidin place, and there was the money, the gold, maps, and detailed records. Hell, boys, even the major smiled. When the major came back up, we put an end to old man Blankenship and his whelp of a kid. But the old lady and the girls await some real men. But first I need a report on where we stand. Cliff, you first."

Cliff was in the group that took the soldiers and the cave. He looks at Badger and smiles, "We got all the rats exterminated in their snug little beds. We cleared the cave and got everything topside we can take. Dennis brought all the slaves over, and they are now sittin in the cave. They're just sittin, and some are sleepin. They're scared as hell cause they got no idea what's happenin. Hell, we brought the dynamite and powder right by where they are sittin, and I swear not one of em even paid any attention. Four of the men loaded the wagons, and we can pull the wagons out here anytime you want. We got a lot of explosives in them wagons, so we need to be sure they're clear of that building before we blow the cave and all those slaves with it."

Badger pauses a moment and then continues, "Okay, you wagon drivers can go upstairs first. Joe and Jack will show ya the rooms. The rest of ya line up in the hallway upstairs and take turns. We ain't got time for each of ya to do all three so make your choice and move on."

Now there was laughing and talking about tonight's conquest. Mickey feels physically sick about what's happening upstairs, so he sits on the porch. An hour passes and the soldiers are laughing and talking louder as they come out the front door telling of who they picked and what special sexual proclivities they brought to the gruesome banquet upstairs. Mickey just wants this to be over so they can get back to camp. He's sure now he wants nothing more to do with this outfit, and his disappointment in Joe leaves him without any reason to care about the consequences of quitting this and returning to his old unit.

Suddenly Mickey is snatched up and bear hugged from behind. A blindfold is put tightly around his head, and though he struggles, he's no match for three men carrying him up the stairs. Two men have him by the shoulders, and one has his feet and legs, carrying him like a pile driver.

Mickey clearly hears Joe's voice, "Here. This one'll be just right for a starter."

Mickey yells out, "Joe, what's goin on? Joe, c'mon, help me!"

Mickey is sure they are going to try to get him to rape one of the girls or their mother, and he will not do it. Mickey's body is tossed around, and he can tell he's being held like a battering ram, head first. Amidst the laughing, he's thrust forward, and his face is shoved onto something at first he thinks is a soaking wet pillow. With the grips released he tears at the blindfold, and it is worse than he could ever imagine. He was put face-first onto the nude, semi-conscious body of the teenage Blankenship girl.

As Mickey recoils backward he can see her bruised and bloody body, caked blood around her mouth and nose and her eyes barely open. At first, he thinks she's dead then she moves a little but makes no sound, at least no sound that was possibly heard above the laughing and clapping of the dozen or so soldiers crowded into the room to watch. Before he can even sit up, Mickey turns his head, and projectile vomits all over the sparkling boots and grey riding pants of Major Breault.

Mickey thrashes his arms and swings his fists wildly into the air. He doesn't care. He has to get out! He has to get out!

CHAPTER 11

CHANGE IN CAREER PATH

Once he breaks free, he runs down the steps amidst the men still coming upstairs. Mickey runs out the front door and gets about twenty feet beyond the porch. He stumbles to his knees and vomits again, but there's nothing in his system so he wretches in what seems to be an unending volley of stomach spasms. Mickey cries out in loud sobs until a hand takes him firmly by the shoulder. Mickey jerks his shoulder away, but the grip returns and is too powerful to escape again. Mickey is turned around and looks up into the face of Badger.

"You don't like us so good anymore...do ya kid?"

Between the sobs, Mickey is able to get out a few understandable words, "Murderers...oh God... what you did to those people...you and your...major...murderers...even my own brother…"

"Shut your fuckin mouth, you snot-nose, little Irish shit. I knew the minute I laid eyes on ya...what are ya? Fourteen or fifteen? Well, you listen to me. Yer in my army and that's that. If you ever talk to me, the major or any sergeant like you just did, I'll horsewhip yer ass within an inch of certain death. Got it? "

Mickey is no longer sobbing, and his anger spills over, "I want away from you and that crazy major as quick as I can. I don't care no more. I'll run away if I have to."

Badger pauses for a moment, looks around to be sure no one but Mickey can hear him. Badger speaks in a low deep voice, "I wondered about you since the day ya arrived. Runnin away will get ya hung or shot for desertion. Maybe I have something better in mind. How about a little time off and let you go visit with yer Ma. Ya know... your homeplace is just about a day's ride from this place. You know that?"

Mickey nods that he knows and Badger carefully looks all around and then quietly continues, "Why don't you take a three-day furlough and go home. You can see your ma, and I can get a transfer fixed up. Then you come on back to camp, and we'll finish everything all proper and stuff. How's that?"

"You'll do that? So I can go home...and then you'll get me transferred?"

"Yep. But I can't have anybody know I treated you so easy, not even Joe. So if it's a deal, you run up that hill, get your horse and get outta here right now. Don't talk to nobody here...just go. You go straight home. And then you get yer ass back to camp by noon of the fourth day from right now. That'd be ...let's see...Thursday."

Mickey doesn't smile, but he manages a bit of gratitude, "Thanks, Sergeant. I'm goin. Hope you're not too mad at me. I just can't do this."

Badger puts his index finger to his lips for Mickey's silence and motions dramatically for him to go. Mickey runs to where he tied Chigger, climbs up and begins a trot and then a gallop as he heads for home. As he reaches the hilltop where this all began tonight, Mickey is tempted to look around to see if the house and barn are on fire, but he overcomes the temptation and keeps riding. First light will be an hour or two, and with any luck, he can be home by late today.

As daylight breaks in the eastern sky, Mickey is seeing familiar territory. Eight more hours in the saddle and he'll be home or very close to it. He's so tired he can hardly sit in the saddle, but he has to be smart enough not to get spotted by any Yankee soldier or sympathizer who might pot shot him or even worse, take him prisoner. Mickey stops at a small creek and lets Chigger have a rest and drink. Mickey bends down to get a drink for himself and sees his reflection. His face and grey undershirt are smeared with blood. He washes his face in the cold water and gets some of the blood from his shirt. When he wrings out his undershirt, tiny thread-like rivulets of blood can be seen in the water, and then they disappear forever.

"Oh, God. I can't believe what happened. That poor little girl. That sure as hell ain't nothin to do with war. Their all crazy. Even Joe's crazy. Not a hero in the bunch!"

He may have washed some of the blood from his shirt, but washing will never erase what's stuck in his memory. Mickey dry heaves again at the very thoughts of last night. It seems like a bad dream, but he can never forget the face and injuries of the Blankenship girl. Tears well up in Mickey's eyes as he knows from the plan that by now all the Blankenship family is dead, all those slaves blown up in the cave and the "heroes" are laughing and celebrating on what a good time they had on this important war mission. Anger replaces his sadness as he imagines the major and Badger leading the convoy of murdering, raping thieves back to camp where they can all continue to congratulate each other.

The last five miles to home, Mickey feels an air of freedom as he walks Chigger along the railroad tracks and then down along the Castor River past the railway station at Cornwall. Soon he's riding up the road toward his home. He hopes his little brothers and sisters will come out to greet him, but it's almost dark, and he can make out only his ma with a shotgun in hand. Mickey takes his hat off and waves his wet undershirt like a flag of surrender at his Ma, and she recognizes him. She props the shotgun against the door and comes running out to meet him.

"Oh, Michael. Holy Mother, praise to you for deliverin my son back to me. I wondered if I'd ever see you again. How I've missed you."

"Ya know, Ma, I got in trouble from that preacher for leanin that shotgun against the door. Think it's safe for me to come home a couple of days while you're in charge of the shotgun?" Mickey climbs down off Chigger and pulls the reins to the front so he can tie them to the porch rail.

Mickey and his Ma embrace and pat each other on the back. Ma pulls back from him a little, "My God, Son...yer pure muscle. I'll fix you somethin to eat, and you can tell me all you've been doing. The kids will be home from school a little later. They'll be so excited to see you."

"It's good to be home, Ma. Wouldn't take me much convincin just to stay home. But I can't really do that. I gotta be back in a couple of days, Thursday noon. So I'll have to leave Wed night."

They spend the evening reminiscing about the family but when questions turn to the war, where he's been or what he's been doing Mickey brothers or sisters get a somber look and a comment like, "Hmmm. Ya know there's some stuff I really can't talk about and then there's some stuff I won't talk about. The war ain't what ya think. It's got some terrible nasty sides to it. Stuff I wouldn't speak about in this house."

The next day after the children reluctantly make their way to school, Mickey and his Ma continue to sit in the kitchen and talk.

"Michael Sean, I just can't get over what a man you've become and you ain't even eighteen yet. Sometime I'm gonna make you tell me who let you into the army being as young as you were...bein as young as you still are today."

"Aw, c'mon, Ma. Ya know I got a major who told me it's my job not to lie to him but he said it's his job not to ask the sort of questions that could put me in a spot where I might lie. Pretty good thinkin if you ask me."

"Thinkin, my foot. That's not a good man, Mickey. He don't care about bein honest, just do whatever suits him. Plum bad if you ask me. I won't do it now, but you'd best believe I will be askin those questions one of these days and it's to hear the truth. I'm fine with the truth even when it hurts. So you better never lie to me, and I'll be askin whatever question is troublin me. I can look right through you...muscles and all."

On the second full day home, Ma whistles and Mickey looks out the kitchen window. Mickey can already tell the identities of the two riders coming slowly on the road to the O'Day house. It's Joe and Badger, but Mickey's a little fearful as to why they're here. They had to have come straight from the Blankenship raid. There's no way they could have been to camp and back. Maybe Joe got a furlough, too. Maybe Badger wants Joe to convince Mickey not to leave Major Breault's unit. Maybe Badger has Mickey's new assignment already set with Major Breault. Well, whatever the reason for Badger's visit along with Joe it can't be anything bad. Mickey comes outside and waves. Joe and Badger stop their horses and talk for a moment, then proceed toward the house. Mickey and his Ma wait on the porch.

"Joe jumps from his horse and runs to hug Ma.

"Joseph O'Day, you are a sight for these sad Irish eyes!"

"Ma, it's so good to see ya! So good!"

Ma, looks at the hulk of a man sitting, unsmiling on the other horse, "Well, Joe, you just gonna leave yer friend sittin there. Hello, sir, I'm Mildred O'Day."

"Howdy-do, Ma'am. I'm just called Badger. Sergeant Badger."

Ma continues in her excitement to have her two sons home...together, "Would all of youse just come on in and let me get ya somethin to eat. Coffee pot's hot and I can rustle up some food pretty quick. How's that sound?"

Badger remains tough looking and expressionless, but he appears to be suppressing what may be a smile, "Oh that does sound good, Ma'am. Home cookin can't be beat. But, Ma'am, after supper the three of us will have to get goin. Real sorry for the short visit for you and Joe but we needed to come by in case Michael was here and here he is. So we'll take a bite to eat with youse and then we have to get goin. Better for us to travel as much as possible at night."

Mickey's mouth is open. What's Badger talking about. Wanted to see if he's here. Of course, this is where he'd be. This is what bein home on furlough means.

Joe smiles, but he looks nervous and figety. Joe avoids eye contact with Mickey.

Mickey catches Joe's arm as he goes past him at the kitchen door, "Joey, what's the matter? You and Badger not havin a good time travelin together?"

Joe jerks his arm from Mickey's loose grip, "Let go, kid. Not now. Just do what Badger and I say." Joe glares at him but doesn't say another word.

After supper, Mickey gets up from the table, goes to the porch, plops down in a rocking chair and is questioning his brothers and sisters about what's been going on at school. Mickey can't imagine how a few months have passed and how separated he is from thinking like a schoolboy. Badger comes outside and asks the kids if he and Mickey can talk privately. Of course with Badger's imposing and unfriendly appearance the kids scatter like rats off a ship.

Badger stands beside the rocking chair and says quietly, "O'Day, I hope you got a little visiting done. We are gonna have to go back to camp right now to get you finalized. So say yer goodbyes and we'll get underway back to camp."

"Why'd Joe come, anyhow? Why'd both of ya come?"

Badger shrugs and looks innocently over both shoulders, "Don't worry about it kid. You wanted out. That's bein taken care of. And don't let your mouth get away from you when yer talkin to me. We ain't big buddies or nothin. You've got more coddlin from me than anybody else, bein Joe's brother and all, but yer pushin it. For now, just go get your stuff, give everybody a kiss, saddle all three horses and bring em up front here. We need to get goin."

For the first time, Mickey sees Badger grin widely, his ugly crooked, brown teeth showing and in a low sadistic growl, "By the way, don't kiss yer old lady or none of them little brood-mare sisters of yers like ya did that little gal back at the farmhouse."

Mickey jumps to his feet, "Aw God. Don't even talk like that. It makes me sick!"

Badger is smiling sadistically, "Geez. I thought maybe ya was developin a taste fer it, Kid, and on the other hand, it'd be a shame if ya kiss yer Ma and then throw up on her." Badger thinks this is the funniest thing in the world and laughs like the sinister, crude pervert he is.

Mickey almost flares up but holds his tongue. He goes back inside, bids his ma and the kids goodbye and gets his saddlebags and bedroll. Mickey's ma makes up a feed sack with some leftover fried chicken. Joe says his goodbyes and Mickey remains puzzled why Joe is so uneasy and irritable with him. Joe generally seems agitated the entire short time he's been at home. Mickey supposes maybe Badger is on Joe's back about something.

Soon, Mickey has the horses up front, and the three soldiers mount, turn the horses and walk slowly away from the house with the tearful waves from Mildred and the children staying behind. Within twenty minutes the three cross Castor River and follow it as far as the path that leads to the railroad tracks, past Cornwall station and further on the tracks. Not a word is spoken since they left the O'Day house.

When it's time to leave the tracks and take the road, Badger pulls up and dismounts. He pulls his horse's reins over its head and hands them to Joe as he dismounts and holds his own horse. Mickey assumes they are taking a little break, so he dismounts and pats Chigger. As Mickey starts to turn around, Badger puts his hand on Mickey's shoulder, "Turn around here, real slow like. Put your hands behind ya, kid. Don't give me no shit or struggle with me. Just do as I say." The major isn't happy with you up and runnin away like ya did. And he's not happy at all with you lyin yer way into his unit and then pussyin yer way out. Soldiers would give their left nut to get into this unit ...and you run away. What the fuck is the matter with you? Chickenshit? Besides, you screwed up his boots and pants... but all that shit aside... he just wants you back so he can personally take care of you all nice and proper."

Mickey reacts without thinking as he snaps his head around and looks at Badger. That last statement didn't sound right." Sarge, whadaya mean by the Maj taking care of me properly?"

Mickey is shocked, puzzled and confused as he shoots a glance in Joe's direction. Joe looks at Mickey with sad eyes and turns his back. Mickey complies with Badger's instruction and handcuffs snap onto Mickey's wrists. Joe continues to stare away from Mickey.

"What's going on? Joe, tell me what's going on?"

Joe stays silent. Badger's big hands grip Mickey's shoulders, and he spins him around like a paper doll. Badger smiles once again, "Kid, outta respect for Joe we made no trouble at your Ma's house. That's a favor to Joe, not ever got by anybody else. Usually, deserters start tryin to make a run for it right off. I'm glad you played along, had a good meal and now we gotta get you back to face Major Breault's dance. Ya know, I really thought you might be cut from the same cloth as Joe but you ain't worthy of wipin his ass. You're just a scrawny-assed, spineless, coward, deserter."

"Sergeant... you, you, you gave me a furlough." Mickey turns to Joe who still is looking away, Joe do something. You know me better than that. I wouldn't just take off and not come back without permission."

Now Joe turns toward Mickey in anger, "Mickey, do you think you're smarter than everybody else? I don't know where you learned to lie, even the word furlough... where'd you ever hear that? Not in our unit. But actin like a spoiled little kid ain't worked so good this time. Lots of men I know and trust heard you tellin Badger off the other night and callin the major names and sayin ya didn't care and you'd just run off...and I reckon that's exactly what ya did. Furlough, huh? In the middle of an operation, a furlough? Sure, Mickey. In a kid's mind but this time you're playin with men...soldiers. You can't play soldier one day, be a kid the next and just quit and go home when it gets tough."

"Joey, I swear I didn't run away. Badger gave me a furlough."

Badger hits Mickey in the jaw, so hard Mickey's feet leave the ground, and he lands on his back with his arms behind him. "To you I'm Sergeant. To me, you will now be known as Prisoner. No other name. There won't be any more talking from you. Prisoner! Silence! You keep tryin to make me out a liar, givin out furloughs, so you don't wanna admit to desertin, huh Prisoner? I'm gonna put you back on that horse, and we're going to get back on the road to go see the good major and your fellow soldiers who trusted you. You just sit up there and say your prayers. Ready Joe?"

"Ready, Sergeant."

The three horses walk at a quick pace on the moonlit road. Joe is in the lead holding Chigger's reins and Badger rides behind. After a few long hours, they leave the roadway and come to a creek. It's a bright moonlit night and not a breeze blowing. Any other time this might be wonderful night to travel but not under Mickey's circumstances.

Badger and Joe dismount. Badger reaches into his saddlebag, brings out a chain hobble and puts it onto Chigger's hind ankles. "There we are. You and that horse ain't goin nowhere at the moment. Joe, c'mere. I need to talk to ya."

Badger walks about twenty-five or thirty feet from Chigger and gets up close to Joe. "I know this is really rough on you, with him bein your kid brother and all. And I know your Ma and them kids will be heartbroken to know what happened, so the major told me to offer you some choices."

Joe looks at Badger, "What do you mean choices?"

Badger shifts his weight from one foot to the other and rubs his chin whiskers, "Choice one is we ride back into camp like we are right now. The major convenes a court martial, and your brother gets convicted of desertion and then hung in front of everybody. But the major wants you to have another choice, too. Think real hard before you give me an answer. In this choice, you shoot your brother...clean head shot, right here and now. He never knows what hit him. We do a little extra slashin on him afterwards, and we take off the cuffs and take him back to camp with a blanket over him. The story is he was a little steamed the other night and simply took a quick little ride to the hilltop above the farm. He was snatched up by a Yankee patrol and when you and me went lookin for him we ran upon this patrol and spotted yer brother. About the time we saw them yer brother went on a rampage-grabbin a Yank next to him, gettin his gun away and shootin the cuffs they had on him and then he proceeded to single-handedly fight his way outta there. He put them yanks on the run just as we were arriving on the scene, but one of the yanks turned and took a lucky pot shot and killed your brother."

"Nobody will believe that."

"Believe me, Joe, I don't do it too good, but the major will describe it so's everybody will know it's the truth. Your brother will be awarded a hero medal posthumously, and that will be given to your ma. You'll get an immediate battlefield promotion to Sergeant First Class, and you'll be second to me, with yer own private tent next to me and the major. You know a couple days from now it's all over for your brother one way or the other, and it's just the major is offering a way to make it better for you and your family. Take a few minutes and tell me what you want to do. Ya know desertin don't get handled too pretty."

"Sergeant I gotta ask ya...was there any mention by you of Mickey gettin a pass or furlough for a couple of days?"

"C'mon, Joe. We don't even use the terms pass and furlough. That's in them regular units. If I let somebody go home a bit for a funeral or somethin like that, everybody knows, and there's no term for it. They just go home for a bit and then come back. Your brother was settlin in. He had no thoughts about comin back. Joe, I truly am sorry that it's yer brother and all, but time's short. Ya gotta tell me yer choice."

"Okay. Okay. Just give me a minute." Joe walks several yards away, head down, pacing aimlessly and shaking his head. Mickey is turned in his saddle looking at Joe trying to imagine what is happening.

Joe returns to the side of Badger and says," You're right. I need to take care of my own family problems. I just need a couple of seconds to talk to him, so I can be at peace with myself."

"Sure, Joe, go ahead. And Joe...it is family, so I'm makin sure nothin strange happens. Got it? I'll wait here. Badger pulls a sawed-off double barrel shotgun from a holster on the left side of his saddle and just in front of his leg. He lays the shotgun across his lap and cocks the hammer of one barrel.

Joe goes over to Mickey and looks up at him. Mickey looks into Joe's eyes but remains silent as he's instructed to do. "Everything will be alright, Mickey. I'm gonna get you outta this and Ma will be really, really proud. I gotta ask ya kid and think real hard before ya answer me. Have you ever lied to me, Mickey? I mean ever in yer whole life? Have you? Ever in your whole life...have you? Just nod yes or no, don't speak."

Mickey nods a negative response as tears roll down his cheek. "Never to you, Joe. I've fibbed to Ma but never, ever so much as a fib to you, Joey...not ever.And Badger told me I could go home. I swear before God." Mickey faces forward. His heart is pounding and his mouth dry. He feels like he's going to black out. He's guessed his fate. He faces forward in the saddle with tears silently rolling down both cheeks.

Joe walks back to Badger's horse and stops on the left side of the horse looking up at Badger. In slow dramatic fashion Badger pulls his personal Henry repeating rifle out of its saddle holster. "I'm even gonna let you use my Sweet Seventeen, Joe. Ya know these here rifles are one in a million. I'm the only man in our unit to have one of these, and it's the least I can do to help ya out by lettin ya use it."

He pulls down the lever and opens the breech, showing Joe the chamber is empty. Badger holds one forty millimeter cartridge in his fingers, and he smiles at Joe, "You come round to my right side and take the gun and the cartridge, walk up there close to the kid and when you're where ya need to be to finish this, then ya put the cartridge in and ya do what ya gotta do. One shot. I'll just sit here with my scatter-gun to be sure we don't have any problems ...you and me or changes of heart."

Joe takes a deep breath and exhales in nervous little gasps showing how difficult this is. Joe looks up at Badger and then walks behind Badger's horse and around to the other side to get the rifle, "Okay. I'm ready. Let's get on with it. Ain't gonna get any easier."

"Atta, Boy, Joe."

Joe mutters as he walks to Badger's right side. "I know, I know."

In one fluid and silent motion, Joe draws the knife from his boot and grabs Badger's right hand instead of the rifle. Joe stabs Badger in the chest so hard it makes a "thud" sound. Badger mumbles in surprise and struggles to turn the shotgun on Joe. Joe continues his grip on Badger's hand and pulls him off the horse. He slices Badger's throat, and the mumbling becomes immediately unintelligible and turns to gurgles and choking. Joe cuts down on Badger's right hand still gripping the shotgun, takes the gun and puts it against Badger's face and pulls the trigger.

KA-BOOM!!

The horses jump at the sound of the shotgun blast but Mickey quickly says something to Chigger, and the horse steadies once again.

Joe is splattered with Badger's blood when he walks toward Mickey, "Okay, Brother. Badger's done, but our troubles just started. I figure we got until day's end tomorrow to disappear along with Ma and the kids. The major will be on our trail, and you don't need to be told what will happen if he catches any of us."

"You do believe me that I never, ever have lied to you in my life?"

"You're sitting alive on your horse ain't ya? Blood's thicker than water, Mick. Soldier-Boy, you and I got some quick thinkin to do. First, we need to get rid of this big pile of steamin shit."

"Ya know, Joe, the first place the major will send guys lookin for us is Ma's house. She and the kids can't be there. You know what they'll do to em."

"Mick! Just calm down for a minute. That's what I just said...and we have no choice. We gotta get Ma and the kids outta there, but you can rest assured when they find nobody home they'll burn the place to the ground and come after us. So let's get rid of this lump of blubber and high-tail-it for home, and get Ma and the kids outta there."

"I'll dig a hole over here by the creek where the dirt is a little easier. Okay, Joe?"

"Don't even bother diggin, Mick. Let's see if the two of us can drag him over that way and we'll put him in the water and just cover him with rocks. Maybe he'll look like a natural part of the stream bed."

Joe pauses and looks at Mickey. A big grin spreads across Joes face, "Ya know, Mick, if he washes loose he'll just dam up the creek downstream and flood out some poor farmer. No jokin though, he's the devil hisself. The dead devil now. What I did was way too good for him, and the major deserves the same. But let's get crackin, Boy. We gotta get home and gather up the family."

"What about his horse, Joe? Take it or let it loose?"

"Nah, we'll take it. Packin the family out has to be quick, and this guy will come in handy. What the hell's horse thievin along with desertion and murder? We can always sell the horse."

Mickey and Joe drag Badger into the creek, and both are still breathing hard as they strip him naked and put his clothes in a pile on the bank. They cover him with the biggest rocks around and return to Badger's horse where they pack his wet clothes and boots in his saddle pack. Joe takes Badger's horse's reins in hand and starts off at a walking pace with the extra horse obediently following on the side of Joe without much resistance to Joe's grip on the reins.

Mickey and Joe pick up the pace and ride side-by-side making plans to rescue and make good their family 's escape

CHAPTER 12

GO WEST YOUNG MAN...QUICKLY!

Joe talks as if he's thinking out loud, "We'll first get out of the house and go West. I wish I knew how to contact Quantrill. Met him once. He's operatin in Kansas. Might offer you and me some protection but then there's Ma and the kids. Breault might use his contacts to find out we were with Quantrill. So maybe that's not such a good idea. Too easy for us all to get found."

"Joe, how much time have we got to get Ma and the kids packed up and on the road? How long til Breault puts two and two together and comes lookin for us?"

Joe is in his own world and ignores Mickey, "Yeah, the more I think about it probably not so good. Gettin with Quantrill might be okay for the two of us but what about a safe place for Ma and the little guys? I think we'd best get across Missouri as quick as we can and bear Southwest down into the Indian Territory and Texas area. That's some bad, bad Indian country but we'll be safer tryin to get peaceful with the Indians than getting caught by Breault...huh? You say somethin to me, Mick?"

"Yeah, Joe. I said how much time you figure we got to pack up Ma and the kids and get away from the farm? One? Two? Three days?"

Now Joe is paying attention, "One thing fer sure. We don't want to make a mistake by a day. When none of the three of us show up in camp, Breault will know

Badger's done fer. He'll know we killed his boy, and he's gonna come after us like a hornet. In fact, he'll have the whole swarm lookin for us. I mean...you've seen what that cold bastard does when it's just an assignment...think about when it's personal to him. Nope, we need to be away from the farm by end of tomorrow at the latest. And we've got to all go by horseback. All of us. No wagons full of keepsakes and shit. We gotta get away fast and keep goin. We gotta stay out of the open cause anybody who sees us and Breault questions will sure as hell tell him. I know that fer sure. Breault will try to think like we do so we got to fool him."

Mickey pulls up Chigger's reins, "That man thinks like nobody I've ever met. He's plum crazy. We just gotta make a run for it. We might not be able to outsmart Breault but we might be able to outrun him."

"And I say we can outsmart him. Now that I think about it, I think Breault will figure we're goin straight for Quantrill in Kansas and that's why it seems to me a better plan is for us to head Southwest straight into the middle of the Indian Territory as fast as we can and take our chances. We'll need to get through the Osage, and I think it's the Kiowas and get into the heart of Comanche territory. I don't know anything about any of them first hand, Only what I've been told. That territory can be like bein in hell from what I've heard. But that's the best chance we got. You and me gotta keep everybody in our clan alive until we can make some kinda deal with the Indians…most likely the Comanches. There are some mixed Mexican and Indian guys around those parts, and I think they call them Comancheros. The Comancheros stay alive by tradin with the Indians and bein nastier than they are. And that's what we're gonna have to do, too. And it'll be rough cause we got the rest of the family to protect along with our own skins. I'll take my chances fightin with the Indians or whoever is out there cause I know there won't be no fight if Breault gets the scent of our trail."

"But what about the guys in the old unit? Maybe they'll drag back a little since you've been a part of the unit and on so many raids with em. And seems to me we can't just start fightin our way West. What do ya do to try to get along? Trade stuff with them? Whatever they're called. If it's tradin seems to me the O'Day clan ain't got much to trade? Half a dozen horses, a mule, a couple of guns? When they're gone what do we trade then? Geez, Joey, this don't seem nothin except a death sentence."

Joe motions for Mickey to catch up to him and not stop, "Well, first off, forget the guys we served with. We're out. They do what they're told by the major. You were the first guy ever in that unit to go directly against the Maj and Badger. I'm the second. We're dead meat to them, and I guarantee there will be some bonus for our ears. That's why they ain't gettin mine, they ain't gettin yours and they ain't harming Ma or the kids. And as far as trade, we'll probably have to do what the Comanches, the buffalo skinners, and the Comancheros do. We'll steal horses. We'll steal guns, horses, and cows. Hell, Michael Sean O'Day, we'll have to start our own raidin party. We'll be like the Quantrills of Texas!"

"You mean the O'Days of Texas!"

Joe laughs for the first time since they were home day before yesterday. They pick up to a gallop headed home. Their plan, good or bad, is coming together.

CHAPTER 13

PACK ‘EM UP, MOVE ‘EM OUT!

Mildred O’Day walks outside at first light to feed the chickens, and she sees three horses, two riders in the distance. She holds her hand to her forehead as if to shield her eyes from the yet-to-appear sun. She’s turning toward the house and the shotgun, but her alarm turns to disbelief as she’s sure it’s her two sons kicking up a bit of dusty trail as they gallop toward the house.

When they are within earshot, Mildred yells out between breaths of excitement, “I swan, you two gonna be the death of me if you keep showin up like this. Maybe you won’t rush off like last time if that big fella ain’t here. I swan, he just ate and was ready to go. Not very friendly if you ask me. What’d he do...go on ahead?”

Mickey slides off of Chigger and walks with deliberate steps toward her, and he is unencumbered by any necessity to sugar-coat the truth, “Ma, we killed him. That guy called Badger. He was gonna have Joey murder me and instead Joey got him. That means we deserted and we’re on the run. In fact, we’re all gonna be on the run as quick as we can get outta here.”

Ma puts her hand over her heart and stumbles back a step for the dramatic effect of shock, “Joe, you get down from that horse and tell me what’s goin on. This is too much to swallow in one bite.”

Joe takes his cap off in a show of respect, "Ma, maybe there'd be a better way to help ya understand but what Mick said is true. Every word. Kids ain't goin to school today, and we gotta be outta here by noon or early afternoon at the latest. "

"Joseph and Michael, you get in this house and start talkin. I know Satin's a loomin cause I feel trouble in the air. Inside and start talkin."

Joe and Mickey nervously sit at the kitchen table and tell their Ma all the gory details of what took place and the impending consequences on all the O'Days, not just Mickey and Joe. The kids stand silently listening as if it's a story and not real.

Ma takes a deep breath, "I had no idea how bad things could get...but if this is what we gotta shoulder...well then, that's what we gotta do. Just so we stay together. This scares me to the marrow. I feel so sorry for your little brothers and sisters. Nothin has been easy on them. Just look at em takin all this in without a word. They've worried about you two and all of us more than you can know...now this. But we'll do whatever it takes, and if we have time later down the road we'll shed tears, but for now, you say we gotta skedaddle."

Joe tries to sort out events, "Okay, Ma. Mick and I got plenty to do so we'll stay clear of the kids until you got them pullin with us. We take no wagons, just horses to ride. The youngins will ride two to a horse. You have a horse to yerself, Ma. Mick and I have our horses. All we can take gotta be carried by horseback. That has to be food, guns and anything worth money in case we gotta trade with the Indians or somebody along the way.

Ma, yer gonna be leavin a lot of keepsakes behind and we likely won't be returnin to get em back. And even if we could come back there won't be anything left when people come through here lookin fer us."

"Yeah, I guess yer right, Joe...for now. But maybe if nobody just outright steals my tin-types and keepsakes...I mean maybe someday?"

Joe puts his hand on his Ma's shoulder, and Mickey turns his back rather than watch her reaction to what Joe's about to say. "Ma, listen to me and I hate to keep harping about how we gotta get goin and who's coming after us but the troops comin to look for us won't leave nothin in their path when they don't find us here."

Mildred grabs her apron and holds it to her eyes. She sobs openly, "Oh God in heaven! My heart will surely break."

Slowly she gets up and walks from the kitchen. Both Mickey and Joe stand in silence as she exits.

Mickey looks at Joe, "God this is hard on her. Joey, it's all my fault. Me and my wantin to be a soldier."

"Too late, kid. That's water under the bridge or Badgers plugin up the river. Our old lady is sad right now but watch her fight for what she knows has to be done. We just need to get busy and get outta here as soon as we can. It'll help if we get started this afternoon and travel tonight. During this first night we can use the main roads fer the most part long as you and I keep close watch. We can't afford to get stopped by any soldiers. All our uniform stuff has to be hid under the food. We gotta convince anyone who stops us that we're movin our family west cause our father just died and left us penniless. If either side finds uniforms and we're wearin regular clothes they'll shoot us as being either deserters or spies. Just as dead either way."

"Okay, let's get on with this. I'll collect all the guns, ammo and knives. How much food you think we oughta take, Joey?"

"I'll tell Ma to keep us all alive for ten days. She can figure it, and I'll have her put it on the table and then we can see how to pack up the mule and the horses."

The swirling preparations to escape have Mickey and Joe occupied completely, and Ma collars all six kids and has them helping with lining up the food. Somehow Mickey thinks Ma has turned this into an adventure for the kids and they seem less anxious about the danger than they are about being away from school and Sarge. They're talking about traveling at night as a family group with Joe and the used-to-want- to be- hero, Mickey, protecting them.

Likely each of the nine people working sees the situation's gravity and danger at different levels. Joe is feeling the pinch as he frequently exhorts Ma and the kids to hurry as fast as possible. Mickey figures Joe is visualizing Major Breault appearing in the doorway and the resulting terror. Mickey saddles and loads the horses and the mule. Slowly but surely the effort takes shape.

Around mid day Mickey and Joe are doing a quiet verbal double-check to see if they've overlooked anything obvious. The entire family gathers on the porch, everything is loaded, and Ma steps forward, "O'Day family, I'm proud of what ya done today.

Staying here is not an option. I'm sad we can't take a lifetime with us except in our memories. I want youse to bow your heads and pray with me."

Ma looks at each of her children, and it's obvious her eyes are glistening with tears, "Bless us oh Lord and bless these gifts, whatever they might be, that we are going to receive. In the name of the Father, Son, and Holy Spirit. Amen."

Brendan laughs when she finishes, Ma, that's what we say before we eat. We gonna eat now?"

Mickey is quick to respond, "Listen, kids, what Ma just prayed we need to remember. We gotta make the most of this, and we'll be blessed when we settle safely. Let's all keep looking forward to that day."

Joe spits and chuckles, "Preacher Michael Sean O'Day and Mother Superior have spoken. Let's saddle up and get outta here."

Joe steps out to his Ma's horse where she's sitting erect in the saddle. "Okay, Ma. This is it. Take the kids and head down to the Castor River under the railroad bridge. I'm gonna be out ahead watchin for anything that could cause a problem so you may not see me all the time. Mick will be ridin behind a bit to do the same from the rear. We'll be a little more together as a group when the sun goes down. Time to get the kids on the move and outta sight of the farm."

Mildred nods, turns her horse and motions for the children to follow. Thirteen-year-old Ailbee has the rope lead for the packhorse, and fourteen-year-old Aileen has the rope lead for the mule. Off go the horses, the mule and nine people from Ma down in age to nine-year-old Colin and Eight-year-old Caireann.

"Okay, Joe. New territory from here on. I'm a little scared but happy to be with ya. I won't ever let ya down, Joe. You're the best brother a man could have."

Joe turns his horse in the direction of the river, "Shit Mick, that's mighty nice of ya, but whaddya mean when ya say that a man can have. What man? You ain't even got peach fuzz on that little cherry face of yours. But thanks. I know ya mean it. And I'm mighty proud to be with ya, and I know how we fight. So I ain't too scared of what we're facin. Just so we're careful cause we got a lot of baggage to take care of headin down the road right now. Just look at em. Oh well, let's take up our points. See ya later."

Once Joe rides past his family group to go on up ahead he's satisfied with the gait as they settle into a quick walk.

The first night is uneventful and just as Joe had hoped. They are able to travel along the main road, and they don't encounter anyone. As first light appears Joe rides back to the group and holds them as Mickey catches up. They move off the road into a gulley concealed by several trees and bushes. They don't have a fire, but all eat some and sleep for a couple hours. Mickey stays at watch over his family.

Before they prepare for the second day of travel Mickey re-enters their sleeping area and quietly explains he spotted a small union supply convoy moving slowly along the road heading east. Mickey returns a second time to give the all clear.

Sundown finds the family looking exhausted already but packing up once again, figuring to get across the Meramec River before daylight.

On night six Joe and Mickey figure they've traveled about two-hundred and fifty miles because they've crossed the low mountains of the Ozarks and should be close to the Osage or Kiowa Indian Territory. From here on, the chances of any regular troops from either side is very slim. They will sleep tonight, and from now on they will stick to the roads and travel in the daylight, making much better time.

Joe has night guard, and Mickey wakes when he hears the clear chattering of a mockingbird- Joe's signal to defend. Mickey springs to his feet, pistol in hand and cocked. On the opposite side of the fire from Mickey stands a rag-tag, bearded man. He has long, coal black hair braided on the sides and doesn't look like what Mickey figured an Indian would look like. He has a pointed nose and displays a big toothy smile. His hands are out to his sides as if to prove he is unarmed.

The man spits into the fire and smiles displaying a partially filled mouth of brown teeth, "Hold it, hold it, Leetle Man. I'm here to help you."

Mickey's Ma is now awake leaning on one elbow and holding a blanket to her neck to conceal the family shotgun beneath the covers. The other children are twisting about but perhaps still asleep, perhaps partially awake.

Mickey keeps the gun pointing on the man, and it's obvious his hand is not shaking, "I don't know who you are, and Mister and I don't know why you're here. You'd best state yer business."

"Hey, take it easy, Leetle Man. I help people who pass this way. I am Valdez."

Mickey uncocks the gun and points the barrel upward, "I reckon the only way you could help is if you know of some small farms or places for us to get started again but way farther West from here. We was barely makin it on a really small place back in Missouri, and then we got burned out by soldiers, my old man was killed, so we come west just lookin to stay outta that war and just get by. Now, is that somethin you can help us with?"

Valdez smiles and spits again, "Look, leetle man, maybe I can help, but I don't want to get shot just for being a nice man. I can think better when I'm not looking at the hole in a gun barrell."

Mickey complies with Valdez's request .

"Leetle Senor, what can you pay if I help you?"

"Well, we don't even know what you can do fer us, if anything. Besides you can see we ain't got much of value… a mule maybe I guess if you knew of a place, but we're goin way on west of here, so that's not very likely."

Valdez laughs a little, then points at Mickey and begins to laugh as if he's just had a great joke played on him. Suddenly he stops laughing and looks directly into Mickey's eyes with a cold stare, "No, Leetle Senor. Do not waste time with me. If you go West, you are in my area for another two days, and I can guarantee safety.

Now you see how Valdez can help? You have several horses, four women and probably guns and money. Valdez just asking what you can pay for safety. There are bad people who are not like Valdez. They might just take everything...and leave nada...you know...no trace of Leetle Senor or his leetle group. You savvy?"

Mickey is over his head real quick, and it's obvious as he lifts the pistol, holding it across his chest, thumb ready to cock it again. He stutters his response, "N' Nope. We'll protect ourselves and be outta your area, as you call it, as quick as we can. So we won't be needin yer help."

Valdez's smile melts from his face. He acts as if he's not even been talking to Mickey, turns abruptly and walks away from the fire without a word, disappearing into the darkness.

By now all the O'Days are out of their bedrolls and standing silently. Mickey motions for them to sit or lie down "Well, that didn't go like I hoped. I have no idea who that guy is or how he came upon us but I really don't trust him. I gotta find Joe. You all just lie down and try to go back to sleep if ya can. Everything's okay. I'll go find Joe. I'm sure he's watching all this."

Mickey walks just out of the light of the fire and Whistles two high, sharp whistles. A few seconds later there's one whistle response. Mickey makes his way in the general direction of the responding sound and soon after he's in the thickness of woods, Joe is right in front of him.

Joe whispers to Mickey, "I think we're okay for the time being, but I think it's best if we get everybody up in a bit and get movin again for the rest of the night. I saw three of them approach, two big-boy Indians and the guy who came into the camp. I saw him take his gun off and hand it to the Indians so I figured he wasn't gonna do anything bad. I also watched when I whistled you the signal, and the Indians never paid any attention so we'll continue to use our same mockingbird signals we know. I'm guessing the two Indians may be Kiowas or maybe Comanches cause they were so big. But I'm not sure. I ain't never been around Indians, so I don't know anything about them. I just want to be sure they don't come back later tonight to take everything, so I'll stay out here til you get Ma and the kids ready. I'm gonna keep circling around right here so it should be safe. Dark, but safe."

"Okay, Joe."

After moving the family about a quarter of a mile and building no fire, they seem temporarily safe in the shelter of darkness. Joe and Mickey both circle in vigilance throughout the night.

The O'Days move several miles westerly the next day. They travel in daylight but are all watchful for anything in the woods beside them. They set up camp again and decide to cook early and extinguish the campfire early. Another night in the dark but probably the safest way to survive at the moment.

The next day, Joe is riding in advance of the family when he sees Valdez ahead just sitting on his horse in the middle of the road. Valdez tosses his cigarette and smiles as Joe approaches. When Joe is a few feet away, he puts his hand on his pistol.

Valdez shrugs his shoulders as if not threatened in the least, “So I meet your leetle man the other night, and we saw you too. You saw my two friends and me, but you never knew about the others watching all the time. It was very smart to move your family in the darkness that night and then no fire last night. Very good. And Valdez is a good man. I watch over your family just to be nice. But, Beeg Man, you are in my woods neck now, and I know everything, and I can do what I want anytime. But Valdez is a good man and can help you...but you must always pay the price. Then all will be muy bueno.”

Joe is shocked that he and Mickey were obviously under false safety for their family. Joe wants to get any dealings over with Valdez quickly.

Valdez knows he has made a realist of Joe at least for the moment, “If we can make a deal I will guarantee your family safety, and I can even take you North to meet Captain Quantrill. You and leetle senor look like running away soldiers to me. Very dangerous. Many people hunt for running soldiers for bounty money. Valdez and my brothers do not hunt for bounty. We provide safe pass. And Valdez can help you. ”

“Yeah, and what about actual soldiers? Yankee? Confederate? Any of those around?”

“maybe, Senor. Sometimes. Soldiers have no place here. My brother warriors like to wear soldier things...you know Senor... hats, swords, guns...and the ears and hair are strong medicine for warriors. My brothers take what they want from white soldiers. Valdez keeps them happy. Most soldiers learn and so not many soldiers come. They afraid to come here. Why...you got a leetle soldier troubles, Senor?" Valdez laughs so hard he coughs several times.

Valdez and Joe ride ahead together and agree on a price of a pistol, a sword and part of Badger's blood-soaked uniform. Joe thinks this is a good deal and they shake hands on it. Valdez rides off quickly, leaving Joe sitting on his horse in front of the approaching family.

"Well, I think we're okay now. I just don't trust Valdez and his Indian buddies. We'll keep headin west and get out of this area. We can always come back over here if we have something to sell and trade. And if we can ever believe we're safe from Breault we'll try to get our name out like Quantrill, so people know who we are. And I was thinkin…maybe later we'll get ahold of one of them magazines on the East Coast. Eastern people are crazy to read about the wild west and some of them magazines send people out to make drawings and write stories so they can go back and sell them. They pay lotsa money if they print them stories. The one thing I know for sure right now, our story will be true, scary and likely full of action before we're settled safe and sound. Jesus, Mickey, you're poison. Now you got me thinkin that hero crap."

"Heck, Joe, That sounds great, but I don't care as much about money as I do bein famous… ya know like a hero. Wow! I'd like to be in a magazine story. Ya know, all this trouble may turn out to be really good."

"Yeah, yeah. But first, little brother, we gotta do one thing for sure. We have to stay alive."

CHAPTER 14

A PLACE TO CALL HOME

The O'Days push on West and are reaching the end of their food supply as they arrive near a little town. As they approach from a distance, their introduction is a board stuck in the ground with some crude printing. The board has an arrow pointing toward town and the words "Broken Feather". They believe they are in the South part of the Indian Territory and maybe as far as Texas. They make a temporary campsite outside of town, and Joe and Mickey ride into town. Joe tells Mickey to go trade one of the oldest pistols for some food. He points Mickey in the direction of the general store, and Joe decides to do his reconnaissance in the saloon.

Mickey walks around the store trying to figure out what will last them a few days. The gentleman who runs the store -bushy eyebrows, no smile, white apron, "Yes, young man, you wish to make a purchase?"

"Yes, sir. We are new in these parts and need to buy some food for the family."

"Before ya go any further. This is cash business, so we don't run no bills to be paid at a later date. So do ya have money to buy?"

"Sir, I have this handgun that is worth fifteen US dollars, and I am willing to trade it to ya for half that value for food in yer store. And I..."

"Get outta here ya shittin little beggar! I deal in cash. Not guns stolen from who knows. Don't come back in here without cash in yer pocket. Now git!"

Mickey exits quickly, and as he gets close to the saloon, Joe appears. Joe has had a couple of drinks and looks optimistically at Mickey. "Hey, Mick. How'd the food shoppin go? You don't seem to be carryin a lot."

"The store man threw me out for just tryin to trade the gun with him. Said we'd have to bring cash to do business there. Is that how it's always gonna be? We gotta take everything to somebody like Valdez and get screwed for the cash. I think they're all in it together."

"In a way, they are, Mick. A man in the saloon told me there's three Comancheros around here and they compete with each other. He also said two of these so-called Comancheros haven't been seen lately and then he laughed. That didn't sound too good. The stores, livery, saloons all pay one certain Comanchero on a regular basis just so they can operate without bein burned out or shot or kidnapped. Ain't none of the stores that will take a trade cause that's what the Comancheros do. Bad system but I think we're safe as long as we know how they operate and we don't try stealin right around here. When we get set up, we'll go north toward Kansas to do any stealin."

Mickey looks bewildered, "So what do we do for food today?"

"Here, Mick. Give me the gun, and I'll get a couple other things outta my saddle bags. Seems maybe the best of the three crooks to trade with is one called Stick. Come on with me and let's see if we can find him.

Always be ready, Mick. We ain't never gonna have nobody we can trust in this place …just you, me and the family. Otherwise, always be on guard."

Mickey hands Joe the pistol still wrapped in the cloth and the two walk down the street toward the livery.

Joe points to a tall, thin man facing away from the O'Day brothers. Three men are talking with the taller man and when they see Joe and Mickey approaching they stop talking and one gives a head nod toward them to give alert to their approach.

Mickey whispers to Joe, "I'll bet that'd be what ever you called him. Stick? Now remember, Joe, we gotta get a place to stay, too. I'm guessin we need food first but we gotta get Ma and the kids put up somewhere and…"

"I know. I know. Maybe if this goes good he'll know of some place, any place, where maybe we can squat with the family for a while at least. Let's see what happens with Stick."

As Mickey and Joe continue to approach, all eyes are on them. The man they assume to be Stick has dark brown skin, well over six feet tall and trim build bordering on skinny. He's wearing shiny boots with fancy silver spurs, what looks like new denim pants and a belt with a big ornate silver buckle. A white shirt and a white broad brimmed hat complete his wardrobe. As the O'Days come closer they can see his bushy black mustache but not a smile or look of cordiality from any. Mickey can't judge the situation. He has no idea whether Stick and his friends will make trouble or if they are simply curious. But that mystery is soon solved.

Joe sticks out his hand, "Senor. I am Joe O'Day, and this here's my little brother, Michael. He goes by Mickey. We're new here and we're pleased to meet ya's."

The tall man stares for a long moment without reciprocating a handshake. He looks at Mickey and then at Joe as if surveying every inch of both men. He pushes the brim of his hat up, still expressionless and with a half step forward takes Joe's hand, "Senor Joe and little senor Mickey. I am Carlos Rodriguez Sanchez Guzman." He holds onto Joe's hand, "Too much words so friends call me Stick." He smiles a broad toothy smile and releases Joe's hand, "And you can be my friends… if you want."

Mickey steps forward shakes hands with Stick and nods to the others.

Stick stands up straight, "You looking for me? Maybe you need help. Stick fixes problems."

Joe smiles, takes a deep breath and tries to lay out what they need, "Ya see, we got our family we're travelin with. This looks to be a peaceful little town and might be a good place to stay for a while. We'd like to get a little place to stay, make a garden, get some chickens…ya know jist a little place. But even more than that we need to get some food for the family today, but that didn't go so good. We're short on cash but the guy over at the general store kicked my brother out of his store for jist tryin to trade a pistol for some food."

Stick holds up his hand as if to stop, "Wait. You talk too fast but I comprehende. Let me think." He takes out a little tobacco bag, rolls a cigarette and lights it as he looks at his silent friends standing next to him. Stick mumbles something to the other men and they immediately laugh as if it's a major joke, but Mickey is almost certain the friends never understood any of the conversation. It was more like Stick told them to laugh and they complied in spades.

An impatient and slightly irritated Joe, tips his hat and smiles at Stick, "Gracias, Senor. But I wasn't jokin or tryin to be funny. We have to take care of our family. I was hoping you could help."

Stick's smile disappears, and he looks menacingly at Joe, "Stop, Senor. Remember…you came looking for me. You have the problem. I don't . You have found Stick. And I told you Stick fixes problems. I am thinking of your problems. Do not worry that my friends laugh. They do not know the English. First, you must know, I am the man who can help you. The food at the store is easy, and I am thinking about as you say, a leetle place to live."

Mickey shoots a worried look at Joe, but Joe takes a deep breath and gives Stick a confident smile, "You're right and I apologize. Take your time. We appreciate it."

Stick continues, "So...we fix the store problem first. What do you have to trade?"

Joe unwraps the gun, and Mickey repeats his sales pitch, "This here handgun is worth at least fifteen U.S. dollars, but I offered it to the store guy and he threw me out. It's worth every penny."

"Little man you are so right. I'll give you fifteen dollars, and you go buy food. Okay?"

Mickey is shocked, "Well sure Mister Stick."

"No little Senor. I no ***Mister*** Stick. I just Stick or Jefe. You know word el Jefe? It mean boss. I Gran Jefe. Beeg Boss. You remember Jefe Stick give you full price. I'm a business man. I give you money for food and you spend in the store. Now stupid store man will have to pay Jefe Stick more money to make up for his mistake. He only takes cash, but he knows to send traders to Stick. Not as you say, kick you out of the store. "

Mickey and Joe get the damp wadded bills from Stick and Stick hands the pistol to one of his friends. The friend spins the cylinder, cocks the hammer and dry fires the gun a couple of times.

Stick looks at Joe, "You have other things to trade soon. Yes?"

"Well, not so much right now but we plan on having more to trade in the future. Maybe a week or so. First, we really need to get our ma and six kids under some kinda roof. We are making a deal to get some horses and maybe some more guns but first things first."

Stick nods, "I know a place. If you want my friends can take you there. Nobody lives there for a long time, but you can stay there, and nobody bother you. Stick can be sure you are safe. Stick is like a brother to Comanches. But you think what you have to trade. You pay me and I keep you safe. Comprehende? You have family and maybe even some pretty little senoritas, no? Stick knows you want them safe. For now, you go with my friends.

They'll show you a place to live. Stick fixes problems but then we must talk soon."

Joe tips his hat, and without a word, he and Mickey start for the general store to purchase food. When they are out of earshot of Stick and his friends, Joe speaks to Mickey without turning his head toward him, "I gotta tell ya, Mick, I don't know how long we oughta stay around here. I have a feelin if we don't keep payin this guy for protection he'll just come with his Indian buddies, cut our goozlers and take everything- and I do mean everything. Probably don't want to ask about people who used to live there. Stop payin Stick and ya become part of the prairie."

"So you think we're walkin right into a massacre? What choices do we have, Joe? Pack up and go somewhere else? I'd say, at least here, if we get some more horses and guns to trade we should be okay. I don't think soldiers will come out here lookin for us."

"Right now I think movin any farther just gets more dangerous and eventually any mistake we'd make would get us slaughtered. It's gonna be the same everywhere we go. That's the price of not getting hung by Breault. I think you and me need to get busy finding some horses and other stuff. North of here...not in Quantrill's neck of the woods, and for sure out of Stick's territory. We need to see how much will buy our safety. I'm really scared for Ma and the girls. For the time bein none of them should ever come into this town."

"Ya know Joe I was thinkin about writin to some of those eastern magazines and see if they'd pay for our story. That'd be easier than stealin. Our name might become famous jest like we always thought and…"

"Are you crazy, Mick? Forget that crap! Right now we ain't got no story. We just got here, and we're tryin to keep our story from becomin how the O'Day family just disappeared. Wiped right off the earth. And we gotta think about not becomin ***that*** true story. If we tell everybody our names and some made up hero story, Breault will figure it out and he'll find a way to have us cut to shreds within a week. Fer now you need to forget about bein a hero, little brother. This is not the time. Right now it looks to me like we might be on the run for as long as we live. And if we can protect Ma and the kids, at least that'll get us a hero badge in heaven. No place else."

Joe isn't looking at Mickey, but if he was, he would see a more dejected look than when Mickey was about to be executed. But dejected or not, Joe is right and Mickey must turn his attention to Joe's advice. It's not the time to be thinking about heroics.

A few moments later Joe and Mickey wait on horseback until Stick's two friends join them. The four head out of town, their horses walking slow shuffling steps. The only sounds in the prairie at this moment are occasional snorting by the horses and squeaking of leather saddles. Not a word is spoken in conversation or attempted conversation. A mile or so outside of town one of Stick's friends pulls his horse to a stop and points to a small mound with a little tree on it.

"Su casa," mutters one of the guides.

Joe and Mickey raise their shoulders in a shrug to communicate they aren't sure what he means or what the mound is supposed to be.

The man looks at his friend and they both laugh. Then he turns back to Joe and Mickey, waves his hand as if impatiently directing them to the mound and says again, "Su Casa."

With that simple statement, Stick's friends turn their horses and begin the slow pace back toward town. They never look back.

Joe and Mickey are confused. They sit on their horses and watch their guides slowly become smaller and smaller as they go out of sight. Joe looks at Mickey, "I don't get it, Mick. What's that little mound with the tree on top? We supposed to build a place out here? Or we supposed to dig a hole in that little hill of dirt and live like gophers?"

"I don't trust any of these people, Joe. I have no idea why they brought us here. I had my pistol stuck in my boot cause I figured they may to try to kill us. No idea why. Just didn't trust em."

"Well, let's ride around it and get a closer look anyhow. I don't get this at all. Keep your eyes open, Mick, in case it's some kinda ambush."

Mickey is silent, but he pulls his pistol into his lap and cocks the hammer. Joe does the same. They begin to slowly approach the dirt mound , going around opposite sides. Mickey circles a hundred feet or so before getting to the edge of the mound. Mickey hollers out, "Hey Joe! Over here!"

Joe pulls his horse next to Mickey and slides to the ground, “Well, I guess then gophers it’ll be. I ain’t never seen nothin like this.”

On the Southeast side of the mound is what looks like the front of a rustic cabin. The mound from the other side is sod piled against the back of the cabin all the way above the roof and there’s a tree growing at the highest point. Joe and Mickey approach the cabin front, guns drawn as Joe uses his foot to push the door open. As it squeaks open, they realize this may not be too bad for a shelter.

Mickey tries to be optimistic, “Well, could be worse…I guess. No furniture, no nothin but I guess we can get some basic stuff to fix it up. A little strange to think there’s only one door out the front. I suppose that means we only got three sides to watch, huh?”

“I ain’t passin judgement jist yet, Mick. I mean here’s what used to be a kitchen, cause this is the stovepipe. There’s a fireplace over there. Looks like three small rooms off the front. Guess those are bedrooms. It might work but I don’t see that dirt piled up in back as protection. I see it as one less escape route should the need arise. Let’s see outside a little more. ”

They walk outside and discover a cistern that likely hasn’t had any water in a while.

“Look over here, Joe. They’ve had gutters and drains for rainwater to get into the cistern. They’ve come loose from the cabin, so that’d at least be one source of water once it rains.”

"Yeah. You're right. I bet we could get a load of water in the meantime and we'll have to get a pump at least to get cistern water. I have no idea if ya can put in a well. Back home we only had to go down thirty-five feet to hit water. I have no idea how deep it might be in this God-forsaken place. Looks like there may have been a well over there, at least at some point. But like everything else at this place, somebody's taken pumps, stove, beds…everything ya need to live. Maybe we can get some secondhand stuff in town, but based on Stick's bargains, we're gonna have to steal a whole lot of horses to get all we need. I guess we can give it a try and maybe get an idea of dealin a little more with Stick. He didn't say no price for this place so we'll have to get that straight real quick. But at least we can get the folks in here tonight and have a roof overhead. We'll need to talk to Stick tomorrow so we don't get crossways over prices and all. We ain't got a lot of choices. Do we, Mick?"

"Nope, not a lot of choices. So what's next? Go get Ma and the kids and show them the bad news here or go get food and then bring em here?"

Joe reaches behind him and pulls a bottle of whiskey out of his saddlebag. He takes a big swig, shakes his head at the shock of the whiskey and extends it toward Mickey. Mickey shakes his head to decline the offer. Joe takes a deep breath and responds to Mickey's question, "Well, let's go back to town, get some food and then we'll collect Ma and the kids and bring em here. We can all bedroll on the floor tonight, but we need to get some plans goin real quick. Can't live long with no pump, no cook stove, no outhouse, no beds or mattresses…tall order, Little Brother."

Mickey doesn't respond, and they both mount up and head at a quicker pace into town.

They make food purchases at the general store, and the owner introduces himself as Samuel Hightower and proclaims a "very big misunderstanding" of Mickey's earlier request to trade. Wherever food is weighed out for their purchase, Samuel puts it to the proper weight and then makes certain he adds a little as he nervously smiles at Joe and Mickey. They inquire about a stove, pump and mattresses. Mr. Hightower would be able to order the items they need, but they carry unaffordable prices because all orders through the store are for new items.

Soon Joe and Mickey are on their way to gather the family and show them the new place. As they near the railroad tracks that go through town, there's added entertainment as a train lumbers toward them from the East. They sit atop their horses eyeing the train's approach and through the belches of black smoke they both spot a familiar sight. There is a big Confederate flag flying from one of the open gondola cars. Joe and Mickey instinctively move to the shade of a nearby grove of trees where they are less visible and can make a run for it if they need to avoid soldiers.

"Shit, Mick, I think we got big problems. After what Valdez said I never dreamed soldiers would come out this far West. This could be really bad. What if they're chasin us?"

Mickey's stomach churns. This is not like being in the army at all. The O'Days have mortal danger coming from every direction and each minute that passes seems to bring new trouble. The train comes closer and soon the engine is even with their position. As they see the rail cars more clearly, once the smoke is past, they are shocked once again.

"Jesus, Mary and Joseph, Joey, it's Indians and a few white guys wearin uniform parts. And they look drunker than hoot owls. They sure as the world ain't soldiers for anybody's army. I don't get that at all. Deserters?"

"Nah, probably not a soldier among em. If I was a bettin man, Mick, I'd say they're returnin to the safety of Oklahoma or maybe west Texas. They musta been doin some raidin of their own. I can't tell ya fer sure, but those white guys look like they might be skinners. There's a place in town they skin buffaloes, and the saloon keeper said there weren't nobody around there these past two weeks. I'm guessin they took some hides and meat back east of here and did a little tradin and some stealin of their own. But ya know what? They sure are enjoyin the booze and uniform parts. Them guys are likely why Valdez said soldiers don't come here. Get yer ass turned into uniform parts. We got some uniform stuff to trade one of these days and come to think of it we might make us a little moonshine to sell. Things might not be all so bad once we sort of think through this. We just gotta get our feet under us…and in a hurry and figure what Stick allows and what he doesn't. I have a feelin that if you do something Stick doesn't allow it isn't a business for very long. That's the facts of life and I guess we need to work our way through it for now. Cause we need to be buyin stuff and tryin to settle in."

Mickey sits silently atop Chigger. After the train is past them, the two slowly proceed toward the family camp.

The homecoming at their new place has mixed reviews. Their ma doesn't have anything to say but looks like she might cry at any second. The kids act excited to stake out a corner for bedrolls and then sstart for the door to go explore outside.

Mildred O'Day is lightning fast with her admonishment, "Listen to me before you cross that door step. You watch your feet for snakes out there. I'm sure there are rattlesnakes and who knows what else. AND…And, you watch for any person approaching. If you see anybody you all get inside real quick til Joe and Mickey can sort it out. Okay, skeedaddle."

The kids have been tethered to campsites for so long they run with a newfound exuberance. They are loudly entertained running up the slanted earth at the rear of the cabin and then running down the sides screaming.

The next morning, Joe and Mickey pack another handgun, a shotgun, a Yankee uniform shirt, and a Confederate army cap and head to town. They soon find Stick and show him the handgun and the uniform shirt. Joe asks Stick point blank, "So Stick, we ain't got hardly nothin but what do ya think these two things are worth? We need food at the store, an old pump that works, a cookstove and maybe some mattresses. Oh yeah, and I know you want some pay for what you said would be for the safety of Ma and kids?"

Stick's eyes are barely noticeable as he looks from under the brim of his hat and squints, "I think you make a bad mistake. Maybe a deadly mistake. That's what I think.

You believe Stick is muy loco. You bring me old guns and a shirt after I was nice to you yesterday to get you food. So you bring these things today... no good to trade. You think you can cheat Stick? Where are horses you talked about? Bring horses...not one horse. Where are the good guns you have? Bring a wagon load...not one or two old guns. No Senor. We have no business today. And you try cheating Stick one more time, and you'll see why Stick's jefe...gran jefe. I have turned people into coyote food for less, Senor. But this is your lucky day, so you listen and learn. Savvy?"

Stick makes a dismissive motion with his hand for Joe and Mickey to leave and then turns his back on them.

Downtrodden and feeling whipped, Joe and Mickey walk their horses a hundred feet or so from Stick, mount up and slowly exit the town.

"Wow, Joey. That wasn't good. I know the stuff we got isn't great but I thought at least it might be okay for a start. Guess I was wrong. That Stick's a nasty bastard. What do we do now?"

"Well, kid, as of this moment, I'd say we're approachin desperate. And ya know we took the worst stuff thinkin we was gonna get something for nothin. Seems Stick ain't a pushover. We got no time to do a proper scouting job, make detailed plans and then steal horses. Time ain't on our side. We gotta focus on two things. First, stay out of Stick's territory to do any stealin. Second, bring Stick some extra good stuff this first time to get off his shit-list. I'm gonna go back and apologize and see if I can get an idea of Stick's territory. Maybe he'd be happy if we steal from his enemies."

After about fifteen minutes Joe catches up with Mickey just before they get to their mound of dirt home. “Okay Mick, I got an idea of how to play this. We’ll hole-up at the farm, have a drink or two and talk it over. Then we’ll plan a ride north up past Black River. Stick don’t go there cause some other scoundrel has that area. The guy is called Moses and Stick just said to steal all you want from Moses but Moses is crazy so best not get caught. He and Stick are enemies.”

Joe continues, “So, we gotta be careful stealin there, and we gotta keep our wits about us, but take whatever we can. We’ll do it as quiet and quick as we can, but if somebody gets in our way, kill em. We gotta be a bit more like Stick and make snap decisions. Somebody crosses us, kill em. As far as hangin offenses we can add horse thievin to the list of murder and desertion. I hate to admit it, Little Brother, but our future is like a storm cloud. We just don’t know when it will be overhead and rain on us. We can do all the stuff we think we can do...moonshine, stealin, tradin...but there are a lot of dangerous shadows around us. Shadows that are just waitin to kill us for looking the wrong way. We got ourselves a good ol Irish curse, and I’m afraid we could be sliding to the end of a mighty bad road. I need a drink real bad.”

“What about bare-knuckle fightin for money?”

“Funny you mention that, Mick. I brought the subject up at the saloon and everybody laughed. One guy said there’s plenty of fights but the prize for winnin is to live another day. The cost of losin is yer dead. Ain’t nobody ever heard of just fightin to see who can lick the other one. These guys bring knives and guns and one wins and one loses. Nope prize fightin is not an option in Broken Feather."

Mickey looks over at Joe, and for once in his life, Mickey sees a man he doesn't know. His real big brother is always the guy afraid of nothing and the guy who someday will make them heroes. At this moment, Joe looks like a scared, dirty, common criminal. Mickey suddenly realizes if he's personally going to be a hero, it will be his own doing, using his own brains. Mickey takes a deep breath, drinking into his lungs the acrid taste of reality. If Joe's too scared, or he gets slowed by drinking then he may not be the guy who can be trusted to take the lead on decisions. Mickey has his doubts that Joe is not likely to be able to pull his share of the load. Being scared or drunk are likely to get them killed or left empty-handed.

That evening Mickey and Joe never discuss their first stealing trip. Joe continues to drink and finally falls asleep.

In the wee hours of that very night, Mickey gets a rifle, a pistol, some bread, water, and three gray blankets. He sneaks out of the house, saddles Chigger and ties two ropes behind his saddle. Mickey sets out due north and rides until mid-morning. He's making good time, and he sees an occasional farmstead that might be worthy of future raids, but for this stealy trip, Mickey figures to go as far north as his time permits and as far as he dares. For sure Mickey wants to avoid stealing from the southernmost farms near the Black River because return trips north will be met with people more alert for thieves like Mickey O'Day.

Mickey is following what he learned from Major Breault's scouts about camouflage. They were experts at stealth, whether grassland or forest. So as Mickey proceeds north, the land is so flat it's difficult to imagine places with any cover to hide behind natural barriers. The secret is to blend into the area. Chigger dutifully lies down and tolerates the gray blankets sprinkled with grass so he and Mickey closely match the local prairie. Mickey finds a spot to rest and observe within a couple hundred yards of the crossing of two fairly-well traveled roads.

In late afternoon Mickey watches a man slowly leading eight horses strung together along one of the roads. As the light of day fades and still staying out of sight, he follows at a distance. Eventually, he spots a little sod house, and it must be the destination of the man and the horses. It appears to be an older man as he moves slowly and with what appears fatigue as he puts the horses in a corral by themselves away from his other horses and cattle.

Mickey is counting on the farmer being worn out from the day's duties. He hopes once he goes to bed he'll sleep sound enough to give Mickey a chance to steal all the horses, the new ones and the ones already at the farm. Mickey patiently waits and watches the house to see if anyone moves or keeps watch out the windows. The eerie flicker of the lamps indoors soon extinguish, and the house is totally dark.

Mickey first slips into the corral with the cows and two horses, secures the horses and leads them along with Chigger over to the corral with the new horses. Chigger and his two new friends provide enough curiosity that six of the eight new horses come right up to the corral fence rails. Mickey slips into the corral and quickly rope-chains the eight horses together. Maybe it's pure luck, but there is not a single whiny or neigh from any of his new herd. Mickey leads them from the corral and leaves the corral gate open, so perhaps the farmer will think they've just gotten out on their own. No matter what the farmer thinks happened, he won't be able to chase very well unless he can ride one of the cows. That will give Mickey plenty of escape time. He leads Chigger and the horses by hand almost out of sight of the farm and then mounts Chigger and begins the way back home.

Mickey rides all night, and by daybreak, he crosses the Black River and is seeing familiar territory. His heart is pounding as he enters the grounds of their little farm and leads the horses up to the porch by the front door. There doesn't appear to be anybody stirring inside the house yet, so Mickey ties Chigger and the ten horses outside the front and quietly enters the house. He's surprised his Ma is sitting by a window, watching.

Ma looks up at Mickey," Morning, Michael Sean."

Oh, oh. His full name is not a good omen, "Morning, Ma. Sleep well?"

"Sure I slept as well as the night you sneaked out and probably helped kill the Hoenisches. You been out murderin again or just stealin horses? You boys are gonna be the death of me. Jesus, Mary and Joseph, Michael, where ***have*** ya been?"

"Ma, I had to go get some horses from some guy up North and I couldn't explain the details before I left."

"Don't you lie to me, Michael Sean. We got no money so how'd you get horses?"

"I won't lie to ya Ma if ya jist ask fewer questions and let me worry about details. So where's Joe? I could use some help."

"Tarnation! I thought Joe was with you. But I'm worrying your brother is going down the same road as yer Pa. He drinks a little all the time and that's too much. Joe left yesterday morning. Said he was goin lookin fer you. He went the direction of town and I ain't seen him since. Do what ya gotta do with them horses and then go try to find him. Ya hear?"

"Yeah, Ma. I hear. I'll try to find him. I'm gonna take four of these horses to town and can you get Ailbee and Breandon to keep these other six from gettin away or gettin stole? They'll need a little feed and water, too."

Michael, you look plum tuckered out. You had any sleep?"

"I'm okay. I got used to sleepin different from when I was in the army with Joey. I'm fine for now."

Mickey picks four of the ten horses, strings them together and starts for town. Just outside of town he glances over to one side and there a couple hundred feet away in a sycamore thicket and as still as five rocks sit five Indians on horseback just watching him. They sit tall on their horses and a guess of size would be well over six feet tall and two hundred or so pounds. Five big guys! One is wearing a union shirt with one of the sleeves missing and one stripe on the other. Another has a blanket over his shoulder and wearing a tattered felt dress hat with a feather in the band. The others are bear-headed. But all five stare intently at Mickey as if cougars watching a fat rabbit. Mickey feels fear to the core of his slight frame.

He pulls his handgun from its holster and makes sure it's loaded, he twirls the cylinder a couple times dramatically checking his gun, and then sticks it in the front of his belted pants. He tugs his hat down tight on his head as he returns the stare. He wants the Indians to see if they attack him they are going to get a fight. He stares at them as he nudges Chigger to continue walking. They never move. After he passes, he turns in his saddle, and they've disappeared.

"Jesus. Those guys is as big as Badger and Groundsie. I don't want a scrap with them."

When Mickey enters town, he leads his string of four horses down the middle of the main street toward the railroad station. Sure enough Stick and a couple of friends are sitting in chairs by the general store. Stick stands and waves when he recognizes Mickey.

"Hey, Little Senor, you come to see Stick to trade now. I can look at your horses?"

"Sure. That's why I brought em. Have a look. Hey, by the way...you seen my brother, Joe?"

Stick looks at Mickey and doesn't laugh or smile, "He's in the saloon. I think he not a good man, Little Senor. You trade with Stick. You better keep all the money. You buy food, you pay Stick for safety, and you buy more horses like these. Buy more horses!" Stick breaks out laughing as he knows these are stolen horses but he jokes that perhaps Mickey bought them.

Mickey laughs, too. "Yep, I figure there are plenty of more horses just like these for sale up North away from your territory.

"These are the best, Little Senor. Young, no brand. Muy Bueno. My brothers and friends who live out of town love these."

"I saw five great big Indians just outside of town. Those your friends?"

"Si. They are big because they are Comanche. My very good friends. They are brothers to me. But only me. You must stay away. Do not try to talk to them, do not run from them and do not act big to them. Leave them alone and everything fine. They listen to Stick. Comprehende?"

"Yep. You won't have to tell me that twice. So how much for the horses? Twenty-five a piece?"

"Oh, you want a hundred. Okay. Stick give you a hundred dollars for all five including yours. Deal?"

"Hell no, that's no deal...Jefe Stick. I'm only selling the four. How much for the four?"

"Oh, too bad. I like your horse a lot. Now, let me see…cause I like the little Senor, I give you twenty for each. Eighty dollars."

"Can't ya go a little more so I can ***buy*** more like these?"

"Oh, Little Senor, I like you. You good trader and good man. Stick very good feeling today. I give you eighty dollars total for the four and Stick get you a stove for Mama to cook and Little Senor…a pump. All for four horses. Only cause Stick likes you. Deal?"

"Deal!"

Mickey and Stick shake hands and Stick pays Mickey seventy dollars and explains, "I keep ten for your family safety this two weeks and next two weeks. After that month, your family doing good and everybody sees. That means it's harder for Stick to keep you safe. So, then fifteen a month. Si?"

"Yeah...si." Mickey isn't overjoyed, but he's satisfied, and he's still got six more horses at home. Stick seems to like Mickey or at least he acts that way. Stick tells Mickey he's going to start calling him Diablito which he says means little devil. Then Stick modifies the name again. He pushes Mickey's hat up and tossles his red hair, "No Little Senor...I make sure everyone around knows my friend, Diablito Rojo. Little Red Devil. You like that?"

"Yeah Jefe Stick...I like that a lot."

They laugh, shake hands and Mickey heads to the saloon and ties up Chigger. He walks through the doorway, and everyone seems to turn and stare.

The bartender bellows, "We ain't selling mama's milk today youngin. This ain't likely the place fer you."

Many laugh but Mickey is focused looking around, "I didn't come in fer trouble. I'm lookin fer my brother, Joe O'Day. Seen him?"

The bartender sounds more civil, "You wait outside, and I'll send him out to ya."

Mickey turns and walks out the door, and the din of men drinking and laughing continues back to normal.

Several minutes pass before Joe comes unsteadily through the doorway to the outside. Joe looks irritated at Mickey, "Let this be the last time you ever come in here lookin fer me. When I'm with a woman I don't like to be interrupted. Besides, what the hell happened to you yesterday or whenever it was?"

"I went north and got ten good horses. No shots fired. No one saw me. Four of em traded fer money, a pump, and a cook stove… ***and*** our safety paid up fer four weeks. I can't wait on ya any longer, Joey. If you ain't got the stomach and straight thinkin to get this done, then it falls to me. Ma thinks yer gonna do like Da done to us. Get to drinkin, seein women and then just disappear. If that's what ya wanta do, okay. I'll handle it at home."

Joe hits Mickey in the jaw so hard it knocks him down, and he feels like he's nearly knocked out. Joe stands over Mickey as he picks him up by his shirt collar, "You ungrateful son-of-a-bitch! You worthless little shit! You can't talk to me like that. Couldn't stomach the Blankenship raid and that little chickadee served up to ya on a platter, and now you think you're gonna preach at me? I sacrificed everything...***everything*** to save yer ass and you're gonna scold me? Not now. Not ever. Now get your scrawny Irish ass up and let's go home."

They walk with Chigger to the livery, Joe gives the stable boy a coin, retrieves his horse and he and Mickey ride silently home. As they approach the farmhouse, Mickey can see Joe straining to see the new horses, but he never acknowledges anything that's taken place.

CHAPTER 15

REKINDLED DREAM

That night Mickey is on night watch, and he pulls a magazine from his saddlebag. He stole it from the Hightower's store as revenge for being shamed and treated badly the first time he was in the store. He tears the editorial credit page from the magazine, folds it and sticks it in his pants pocket. Mickey feels a sense of excitement simply by being in possession of a source for the Atlantic Monthly Magazine.

Mickey smiles and says aloud, " Diablito Rojo. Diablito Rojo!"

The next morning Joe heads to town early, and Ma is upset because Joe took all but a few dollars of the family money. Mickey assures his ma that he'll go find Joe and try to get both Joe and the money back home.

As Mickey gets to town, he sees Joe at the livery apparently borrowing a wagon to haul the pump and stove. Mickey is relieved, and his thoughts immediately turn to the magazine address in his pocket.

Mickey rides to the end of the street that dead ends into the train station. He tethers Chiggar to a hitching post and enters the lobby of the station. The only person in the place is a man with his back to Mickey. He has a black billed cap, a black vest over his white shirt and black pants. He must be the station master so Mickey addresses him, "Excuse me, Sir, I have need of getting a letter back East. Are you the person that can help me do that?"

"I sure am. I can send telegrams or post letters…all confidential of course. So let me see the letter."

Mickey continues, "I ain't got the letter written yet. Ya see, we just moved here, and I got no pen or paper. Where could I get that? Do I have to buy it at the general store?"

The station clerk smiles at Mickey, "Heck no, Son. I got paper and pen and ink here, but it'll cost ya two bits for three sheets of paper, envelope, pen, and ink, ***and*** maybe some of the postage to send it. That's dependin on where it's goin as to how much postage ya gotta pay."

"Well, that sounds jist fine. By the way, I'm Mickey O'Day and my family is stayin out at what Stick said is the old Henson place. I guess they moved and ain't comin back, so we're sort of takin it over right now. And here's two bits for the paper and pen and such."

The clerk looks at Mickey, shakes his head a little and disappears into his office. A couple of minutes later the clerk re-enters the train station waiting room and motions for Mickey to come over to a table by the window. The clerk sets the writing supplies on the table and starts to walk away.

He pauses, turns and comes back to the table. "Son, my name's Ned Hartman and I been here about seven years. This here's a rough town unless ya constantly pay attention to stayin alive. The Hensons didn't move no where, but you're right about one thing. They sure ain't comin back. Word is they cheated or held out on Stick, and a couple of weeks later they just disappeared in the night. But make no mistake of what happened. One of the Comanches that's Stick's friend wears an old uniform shirt that Henson used to wear around town. Another one has strips of cloth hangin from his horse's halter. Sure enough, it's one of the dresses Miz Henson was seen in. Just be careful, Mickey O'Day. This here's a rough place. Don't get in no fights, stay on Stick's good side, and life can be jist fine. You don't tell nobody outside yer family what I jist told you. Ya have a right to know. Now, you write your letter, and I'll help ya get it ready for the post. It can go out tomorrow on the noon train goin east."

"Thanks, Mr. Hartman. I take to heart what ya said, and I think we'll do fine stayin all peaceful with everybody."

Mickey slowly writes a letter and copies the address of the editor of Atlantic Monthly Magazine in Boston. Mickey's letter simply says he's not a writer but he has a true story of the West and the daily heroics of a boy turned man by the war and now raider, Indian fighter, and family protector. He claims to be widely known in these parts as Diablito Rojo.

When he's finished, Ned Hartman takes his letter and adds it to the canvas bag ready to post the next day. Mickey heads home, assuming Joe will be proud to arrive with the supplies for the house. The rest of Mickey's day is filled with thinking bits and pieces of truth that are very brave and exotic should a writer for the magazine ever contact him to hear his story. Mickey imagines that if he gets to tell the story of Diablito Rojo to an east coast reporter, he'll indeed be famous. Horse-thieving can be emboldened into fictional heroism of single-handed fights with Comancheros.

A week passes as the O'Day family works on a garden and stabilizing the makeshift fences and corral. Mickey always volunteers for the occasional trips to town for supplies but mostly to check with Ned to see about any response to his magazine request.

Then it happens. On one of Mickey's trips as his expectations are sinking on a daily basis, word spreads as he arrives in town and a runner with a telegram is sent to find him. Mickey is unfamiliar with telegrams, but this one is not difficult to decipher.

To Michael Sean O'Day stop editor's rep to record your story stop arrive

By train Wed, May 22 stop if you accept we will pay you one-thousand dollars upon writer's approval of your story. stop

James Thomas Fields, Editor, The Atlantic Monthly.

Mickey is so excited he can hardly stand it. His next challenge is to convince Joe that his story will not get them all executed.

That same evening Mickey summons everyone to remain at the table after the evening meal. Mickey explains that the publication will be perfectly safe as he will be sure the name of the town is fictitious. Joe is hesitant to agree, but the thousand dollars sways his decision.

Everything at the O'Day farm seems to be leveling out, and the family is settling in and making the place as homey as possible. Mickey continues to trade occasionally with Stick, and the family's worries about safety seem to be a thing of the past.

On May nineteenth the O'Days are ready to sit down to their evening meal when Joe notices five Indians sitting on horseback about a hundred yards from the front of their house. Mickey moves to the front window.

"Joe, those are the same Indians I saw on the way to town a few weeks ago. Ned Hartman is sure these are the ones who killed the people who used to live here. But Mr. Hartman also said the people who lived here cheated Stick. So we should be fine on that count."

" Well, I don't trust bein looked at like this. We should probably act like there's nothin wrong and sit down to eat but keep pistols on our laps and listen real careful."

The O'Days sit down to eat, and a few short moments later there is a knock at the door. Joe and Mickey are ready with their pistols and Joe sends Breandon to answer the door. Breandon opens the door to a very tall husky Indian, a Comanche by the appearance of clothing, standing at the doorway. With the door open it's obvious the other four Indians are standing on the front porch behind the one in the doorway.

Joe and Mickey both jump to their feet, guns drawn and Joe pushes Breandon away from the door.

But the Indian raises his arms as if in surrender and speaks very softly considering his size, "Stick friends. You safe. Hungry."

The scene is frozen momentarily and not a word is spoken. Then Joe takes an audible deep breath and uncocks his gun. Mickey does the same.

Joe has had a few drinks of whiskey and his defenses not as acute as times past, “Ma, we got enough to share? I think they don’t want trouble. Probably just hungry. These are big guys and look like they can put away a lots of food.”

Ma forces a nervous smile, “Sure. We can scoot around and make room. Seems friendly enough to me, don’t you think? Maybe they’re getting used to us being here.”

Mickey doesn’t say a word. His instincts tell him something isn’t good, but this can become part of his hero-story for the reporter. Joe motions for the Indians to enter and sit at the table. The five squeeze in around the end of the table closest to the door. They are bare-chested as they sit down but each puts a light blanket around their shoulders, almost like a shawl. Ma takes a deep breath and relaxes as she sees this as a sign of respect.

The entire table of food and all that was left on the stove is consumed over the next few minutes. The Indians were certifiably hungry but show no emotion as they finish their last mouthful. When finished eating the Indians stand and head out the door. The one who first came to the door turns and repeats the words, “You safe.”

With that comment, they close the door behind them and walk to their horses. They mount the horses and slowly walk out of sight as darkness sets in. The O’Days animated talking for the rest of the evening is fueled by the release of nervous energy.

Ma's comment is indicative of the more relaxed feelings, " Ya know boys, a few weeks ago I couldn't draw a breath without looking over my shoulder. Now I feel like we are accepted and we may have a life to rebuild right here."

"I think you may be right, Ma. A future life on this prairie may not be so bad. Perhaps we can expand this little homestead and make it as good or better than what we had back in Missouri."

This is one of those nights where the moon is bright and later when all the lamps are out and the house silent, five large, shadowy figures stealthily return to the O'Day farm.

On May 22nd, the train makes its half hour water replenishment stop in Broken Feather, and Everett Holmes, a man in his thirties, exits the train. Everett is in a brown wool suit and wears a fedora. His appearance, if not comical, is at the very least unusual in this little town. Stick is present at the station as are his usual town buddies. Off to one side, nearly out of sight there also is a formation of five large Comanche Indians sitting on horseback.

Everett Holmes looks uneasy and awkward at this welcome and isn't sure if he should quickly retreat to the train or if this is what always happens in the wild west. Stick comes up to Everett.

"Senor, you looking for my friend, Little senor, Diablito Rojo?"

Everett's voice comes out raspy and uncertain, "Yes sir, I'm Everett Holmes with the Atlantic Monthly Magazine, and I'm here to see Michael O'Day and the O'Day family."

Stick is very friendly, "You bring little senor lots of money? Si? He told me to collect it and so you give it to me now and everybody will be very happy."

Everett bristles at Stick's brazen attempt to get money, "I don't know who you are, Sir, but my business, if any at all, is not with you but the O'Days. And certainly I'm not in possession of ***any*** money. I don't see that it's your affair, but we do not carry money around and give it out. It is paid after we accept a story. Then it's done from one bank to another. Now, Sir, do you know where I can find Michael O'Day or can you direct me to someone who will know?"

Stick clenches his fists, takes his hat off and spins around with his back to Everett. He growls a low pitch and then takes a very dramatic deep breath. Now composed, Stick turns toward the five Indians. He addresses them in the Comanche language and then turns back to Everett. The five Comanches move slowly until they are right next to Stick.

Stick takes a step closer and leans forward so he can talk privately to Everett in a seething , sarcastic tone, "So sorry, Senor. No more O'Days. No more. They all move away someplace. Little house empty. No horses, no clothes, no stove, no water pump. Just disappear. My friends here don't know why they would do such a thing."

Stick motions his head to guide Everett's attention toward the Indians. Everett suddenly takes a step back and gasps when he understands what has happened. One of the Indians is wearing a Confederate uniform shirt with Sergeant's stripes. Another has a military sword and is wearing a Union Army cap with a human ear tied to it by a leather thong. He sits atop a beautiful reddish horse, and the blanket is a Confederate saddle blanket. Hanging like a necklace or small breastplate around his neck is a human scalp of red hair strung on a thong. Another has dried bloody handprints all over his chest and one on his forehead. He has a girl's long, light blue blood-soaked dress draped over his horse's mane.

Everett's reaction is obvious, and he is certain what has taken place. These people have killed the O'Days and planned to rob him of what they thought would be a thousand dollars or more. He turns back toward Stick and Stick laughs, "You have no money. You waste time. You waste Stick's time. Best you not look for them, Senor. Best you leave now on this train you came on. Not wait in town for return train. You leave now, Senor. Go on West from here and find another train home. You need to leave here before Stick gets mad with you. Savvy?"

Everett doesn't even respond to Stick. He grabs a pad and pencil from the station master and scribbles a note and shoves some money into Ned's hand, "Sir I trust you can telegraph this for me. This should be enough money to cover it."

Everett quickly re-enters the train car and gives cash to the conductor.

The train whistles and slowly pulls away from the stop.

Stick turns to the station clerk, "What words he want your clickey click to say?"

The station clerk looks nervously at Stick and reads aloud, "Dead story. Stop. Heading home. Stop."

Stick shrugs his shoulders, "Dead story, huh?"

He laughs and walks away. The Indians turn the obedient Chigger and the other horses and walk them past a wagon loaded with an old cook stove, a water pump, saddles, bedrolls, and a few canned goods from the Hightower General Store.

A dust devil sweeps a column of dust skyward, perhaps in tribute to a legend that might have been. And then the sky clears.

Made in the USA
Columbia, SC
28 February 2024